'What's that?' Bethany said, pointing up into the branches of the nearest apple tree.

'Mistletoe,' said Mike knowledgeably. 'People kiss under it.' And he kissed his daughter on the forehead.

Bethany was charmed. 'Grace kiss me now,' she demanded.

So Mike put her down and Grace bent to give the little girl a hug and a kiss.

'Now Grace and Daddy.'

There was a tiny silence. Grace straightened up. Her eyes met Mike's.

'Absolutely,' said Mike. He put one hand on her upper arm and moved forward. Just the most delicate touch of lips on lips. They were cold, but a thrill passed through Grace that she had never quite felt before. She rested one hand on his body, felt the fast beating of his heart through his coat and leaned forward. He kissed her again, warmer, slightly longer, but just as soft. 'For luck,' he said. Then let out a breath, hoisted his daughter up to his shoulder, and walked back to the car.

Gill Sanderson, aka Roger Sanderson, started writing as a husband-and-wife team. At first Gill created the storyline, characters and background, asking Roger to help with the actual writing. But her job became more and more time-consuming, and he took over all of the work. He loves it!

Roger has written many Medical™ Romance books for Harlequin Mills & Boon. Ideas come from three of his children—Helen is a midwife, Adam a health visitor, Mark a consultant oncologist. Weekdays are for work; weekends find Roger walking in the Lake District or Wales.

Recent titles by the same author:

THE COUNTRY DOCTOR'S DAUGHTER
THE MIDWIFE AND THE SINGLE DAD
A MOTHER FOR HIS SON
NURSE BRIDE, BAYSIDE WEDDING*

Brides of Penhally Bay

CHRISTMAS AT RIVERCUT MANOR

BY
GILL SANDERSON

First published in Great Britain 2009
Large Print edition 2010
Harlequin Mills & Boon Limited,
Eton House, 18-24 Paradise Road,
Richmond, Surrey TW9 1SR

© Gill Sanderson 2009

ISBN: 978 0 263 21092 7

Harlequin Mills & Boon policy is to use papers that are
natural, renewable and recyclable products and made
from wood grown in sustainable forests. The logging and
manufacturing process conform to the legal environmental
regulations of the country of origin.

Printed and bound in Great Britain
by CPI Antony Rowe, Chippenham, Wiltshire

CHRISTMAS AT RIVERCUT MANOR

To Oliver and Joe, latest grandchildren.
Have a good life.

CHAPTER ONE

DISTRICT NURSE Grace Fellowes looked at the patient in front of her with mild exasperation. The trouble with these moors farmers—even ones like Albert who'd long since handed over the reins to his son—was that they thought if they slowed down for more than a few minutes they'd be dead. She put on a severe expression. 'You've been walking on this leg, haven't you?'

Albert shifted his ulcerated leg irritably on the footstool. 'Give over, young Grace. As if you haven't already found out from my boy that I just stepped down to the barn to run my eye over the flock and a sheep got in my way.'

'I'm not young Grace today, I'm your nurse and I know what I'm talking about. One in fifty people over the age of eighty get ulcers like yours and because of your blood-pressure problems there isn't enough new blood getting to the tissue to repair it very quickly.'

In truth, almost the only hope with venous ulcers was to dress the wound and then cover it with a compression bandage, but Grace didn't mention that. 'We've kept the germs out so far, but you must be more careful when you move about. Your son's right to be worried about you. How does your leg feel now?'

'Not too bad. Sometimes it itches, sometimes there's a sort of heavy feeling.' He watched as Grace dusted on the dressing, then covered the ulcer with an antiseptic pad and eased on the elasticated support stocking. 'Thanks, lass. That's tight, but I can feel it working. Still seems odd, you junketing all over the moors to see to us. Who'd have thought twenty years ago that young Grace Fellowes from Rivercut Manor would grow up to be our district nurse.'

Grace stood, went to wash her hands in the sink at the side of the farmhouse kitchen and then put on her fleece jacket. 'Be glad I am,' she said lightly. 'You might have a fearsome stranger telling you off instead. I'll be back in a week for another look. Any problem before that—give me a ring. And don't go banging into anything!'

'I suppose,' said Albert. He hesitated. 'Before you go—I'm sorry you've had to put the old place up for sale.'

Grace swallowed. 'Ah, well. That's life. I'm luckier than most. I've got a job I love, a cottage that needs hardly any housework and the nicest patients in the world.' She blinked to clear her eyes and walked quickly to the farmhouse porch, slipping her feet out of her comfortable flatties and into her Wellingtons. It might look a bit odd—a nurse in a smart blue uniform with rubber boots up to her knees—but in most farmyards it was necessary even when they weren't ankle-deep in snow like today. A couple of quick words with Albert's son and then she was back in her car.

As she drove through the high moor tops Grace grinned. 'Young Grace from the Manor' indeed! When was Rivercut valley going to emerge into the twenty-first century? It was a bit isolated—but not that much. You could get to London from York in three hours. Then she chuckled. Provided you could get to York at all with the

North Yorkshire moors snowed up as they were at the moment.

The back road she was on dropped down into a narrow valley. She slowed, seeing that the surface ahead was covered in water. This often happened in winter—the drain under the road was just not big enough to cope with the stream that ran through it. It was fortunate that Grace had grown up here and knew all about the local hazards. Her elderly Land Rover only skidded a little as she carefully drove through the flood.

Climbing the hill again, she caught her breath at how beautiful the countryside was with its blanket of white. Snow had come very early this year—this was only the beginning of December. And the forecast was that the snow was going to last. She knew a cold winter would cause trouble but they were used to it round here. Garages would be stocked with snow chains and anti-freeze, dispensaries would have supplies of cough linctus and crutches.

Grace's next call was at a village called Nestoby. Not that anyone in the large Leeds nursing college where she had done her training would have called it a village. There was only a handful of houses, no pub or post office, just a corner shop that sold an incredible range of goods even though it was situated in the front room of a cottage.

Mr and Mrs Kipps ran the shop—and had done for the past forty years. They'd taken it over from Mrs Kipps's parents. Grace parked outside, opened the shop door and was greeted by an outburst of coughing. She looked at the wizened figure bent double behind the counter. 'Not doing very well, are we, Mr Kipps?' she asked sympathetically.

Mr Kipps was suffering from emphysema. He had smoked all his life until he'd had a bad attack of bronchitis which had laid him up for months. Even so, James Curtis—the GP Grace worked for—had had to put the fear of God into him before he had been persuaded to stop. Now Grace called in regularly to check up on Mr Kipps's condition and to arrange for physiotherapy visits to drain his lungs of fluid.

Mrs Kipps came through to look after the shop. She was a large, unsmiling woman and as a child Grace had found her rather frightening until she had realised her bark was worse than her bite, and most of that barking was directed at the lads who were intent on getting tuppence out of their penny-worth of sweets. 'I'm sorry about the manor,' Mrs Kipps said abruptly now.

Grace gave a rueful smile. 'Thanks, but it's the way of the world. I just hope I can sell it to a family who want to make a home rather than to some faceless company to use for corporate entertaining.' She followed Mr Kipps into the back room to take his blood pressure, listen to his heart and check up on his general well-being. His condition was as good as could be expected for a man who had smoked forty a day for more years than the twenty-eight Grace had been alive.

'How are you feeling?' she asked. 'Not too much pain from the coughing? I know these cold days must be hard on you.'

A voice came from the shop. 'He came home late last Wednesday with the smell of tobacco on him. Told me it was because he'd walked home with one of our neighbours who smokes. I told him that if I found him with a cigarette in his mouth, he'd be out on the moors all night with only his cigarettes to keep him warm.'

'I wasn't smoking!' Mr Kipps wailed.

Grace decided to say nothing. The situation appeared to be under control.

Outside it was snowing again, the hard small snowflakes that landed and settled adding another layer to the smooth, soft outlines of the winter landscape. Grace loved the way snow turned the moors into a whole new land, more beautiful even than the myriad greens of the heather and scrub. She could forgive it making the drive to her last call of the day tricky. She noticed that the Christmas spirit seemed to be abroad. All the isolated farmhouses on the way to Fellowes Top had illuminated Christmas trees in the windows. Grace felt an excited wriggle inside her at the sight. She did love Christmas.

At Fellowes Top Farm she made short shrift of Young Jack Stanley (so called to distinguish him from Old Jack Stanley, his father), who seemed to think that the proper care of a pitchfork wound in his upper leg so deep that it had only just missed the femoral artery was to sweep up slurry in the pigsty. Leaving him chastened, she set off for home. It was a longish journey, Fellowes Top being the most outlying of the properties her family had once owned, but Grace quite liked a drive at the end of a good day. It gave her a chance to unwind from the busyness of health issues resolved and problems fixed.

It was dusk now and the snow was still falling. Grace's dashboard thermometer indicated that the temperature was well below freezing. She snuggled further inside her warm fleece as she drove, thankful that the Land Rover had four-wheel drive. She really must make room in next week's schedule for a service. Maybe Bert Machin wouldn't charge her too much, especially as he would also have heard about the manor going up for sale. Grace bit her lip. Everybody this afternoon had mentioned it, saying how sad it was and how brave Grace was being. And Grace had smiled cheerfully and uttered platitudes and hadn't admitted once that it was tearing her apart to have to sell her childhood home in order to pay off the twin burden of death duties and her mother's debts.

She blinked back tears and concentrated on the road—and realised with a spasm of alarm that she'd automatically chosen the shorter cross-country route home from the farm instead of the gritted main road. Oh, heck, she'd really need her wits about her now. Still, she'd driven along part of it earlier and it had been okay. She'd just have to be extra-careful.

She was miles from the nearest farm when the accident happened. She was taking a right-angle bend, not at all too fast, when the rear wheels broke away and slid sideways. She couldn't believe it! She did everything correctly, didn't over-steer, braked very gently and steered into the direction of the skid. All to no avail. She was coming off the road.

At quite a slow speed the Land Rover slid backwards. There was just a moment when Grace felt completely helpless, then a jerk as the back wheels dropped into a ditch and her head whiplashed forward. The engine cut out. The car was still. *Oh, no,* she thought.

For a minute she simply sat there stupidly, her headlights pointing upwards at an odd angle. *Shock,* diagnosed a detached, professional part of her brain, and with that she clicked back into being Grace Fellowes, District Nurse, again. No part of her was injured, that was good. She was facing the right direction, also good. She had four-wheel drive. With any luck she'd simply be able to drive out.

She took a deep breath and started the engine again. The car lurched forward a couple of feet and then slowly slid backwards. She could hear the whirring of the wheels skidding in the slush of the ditch. *Grip,* she told them, *grip.* Then she remembered that at her last MOT the mechanic had told her the tyres were only just within the legal limit and had nothing like the traction that they should have. Buying new tyres had been a luxury she had been putting off.

She was not going to panic. She turned the lights off to save the battery, took out her mobile to call the garage, remembered—irrationally—that she'd once seen an adder slither out of one of these ditches and cross in front of her and decided she'd get a much better signal on the road. So she clambered out of the car, *not* thinking about snakes, and took a large step up the side of the ditch.

Under the snow it was more slippery than she'd expected. She lost her footing, fell on her knees then pitched forward. Her phone flew out of her hand into the slush and the mud. No! Grace scrabbled frantically for it, but when she eventually closed her fingers around its solid, comforting form it was obvious that no way would it work.

It was as much as she could do to bite back a sob. She felt bewildered. All this had happened so quickly, so easily, that she was having difficulty in comprehending it. Not ten minutes ago she had been happily driving through the snow-covered landscape, looking forward to getting home. And now she was stranded on a lonely country road, she was covered in mud, the light was failing, she had no means of calling anyone and it was at least three miles to the nearest farmhouse. What had happened to her good day?

Another deep breath. This was simply shock. Think positive. She had a torch, she knew exactly where she was and there were worse things in life than an early-evening walk in the snow.

But before she could take a single step she saw lights in the dusk ahead. Oh, thank goodness. What a stroke of luck! A car was coming this way. She stood on the side of the road and shone her torch across it, preparing to wave the driver down.

The car was travelling quite slowly, its engine a muted mutter. She waved vigorously. The car's lights flashed, telling her she'd been seen. Then it drew up to her and stopped.

She recognised the make of car, a top-of-the-range Range Rover, just the kind of vehicle she would love for herself. Hard on that came a momentary touch of apprehension. She knew most of the people around there and none of them had a car like this. The car was driven by a stranger.

A man got out. 'Are you all right?' he called.

'Yes,' Grace called back, 'but I've slid the road.'

'Just a moment.' The man opened one of his rear doors and a minute or so later fetched out a powerful torch. He walked towards her, snow-flakes falling through the beam of light playing on the ground.

'You've had an accident?' he said. 'Are you hurt? I'm a doctor.'

'It's all right,' she said. 'I'm a nurse myself. I'm not hurt, just annoyed and feeling a bit stupid. Not only have I skidded into a ditch, I also dropped my mobile into the slush and it's stopped working.'

'Ah. Then you'd better be careful. Accidents always seem to happen in threes. Think carefully, what else could go wrong?'

He had a gorgeous voice, deep and comforting. And now he knew no one was hurt, it held a touch of humour too. She felt as if she could listen to it for ever. He was probably a consultant, Grace judged, by the expensive car and the fact that he must surely be on his way to join some country party at a big house or a hotel. 'Nothing more will go wrong,' she told him firmly, feeling more cheerful by the moment. 'It's nearly Christmas and I won't allow it. But if I could just borrow your mobile to ring the garage…?'

He chuckled. 'What's the number? Are you cold? Would you like to wait in my car while we contact them?'

'I'm fine, really. Oh, damn.'

'What?'

'The number of the garage is in my phone.'

'Ah, that would be the phone that doesn't work?'

'Yes.' She took a breath. This was perhaps a bit much to ask but he could always refuse. 'Could you give me a lift to the nearest farm? It's only three miles down the road.'

'Certainly I can, but won't they mind?' He sounded startled.

Grace stared at him in the dimness. This was

definitely no local. 'No, of course not! They'll either ring Bert Machin for me or start up the tractor and haul me out of the ditch themselves.'

'Goodness. Well, hop in.'

But as she approached the large, powerful Range Rover, an idea occurred to her. 'Or we could maybe get the tow-rope out of my boot and use *your* car to pull mine out. That would be even quicker.'

He seemed startled again. Grace was reminded once more that he wasn't from around there.

'Sorry,' she said. 'You're on your way somewhere. A lift to the farm would be lovely, if you really don't mind.'

'It's not that.' He looked towards his car as if undecided, then the dark head nodded. 'Yes. If yours isn't damaged, that sounds like a good idea. Just wait there a minute.' He strode along the edge of the ditch, shining the torch at the Land Rover's back wheels. 'Seems possible to pull it out,' he shouted. 'I'll have a quick look at the front.'

He rejoined her, having apparently been able to carry out his inspection without getting anything like as muddy as her. 'I think we should be able to manage it,' he said. 'Sorry I didn't suggest it straight away. I'm not used to owning something this practical yet—even though that was the reason I bought it.'

It seemed a bit extreme, buying a Range Rover just for a trip across the moors, but that was consultants for you. 'That's very kind,' said Grace. 'I'll get the rope. Hopefully this won't hold you up for too long.'

'Don't worry, I bought a rope along with the car. There's even a section in the manual about pulling vehicles out of ditches.' He was hurrying back, peering through the window and reaching around vast quantities of luggage to get shiny new tools out as he spoke. Grace couldn't escape the thought that he probably imagined her towrope was as elderly as the Land Rover. 'I'm Mike, by the way.'

'Nice to meet you. I'm Grace. If you give me the rope I'll fix it to my—'

'Certainly not. This is a new experience and I want to see the whole thing through myself.'

With a touch of laughter in her voice, Grace asked, 'Not because I'm a woman and you're a man?'

'Ah, very possibly. I can on occasion be a slightly unreconstructed male.'

'I've met my share of unreconstructed males, Mike. I don't think you're one of them.'

Had just a touch of bitterness crept into her voice then? She hoped not. She had meant to copy his light-hearted tone. She felt, rather than saw, his sudden assessing glance.

'Perhaps I've been reconstructed just a bit,' he said. 'Tell you what. You can hold the torch and tell me if I'm doing it right.'

His hands, though they must be as cold as her own, were deft and sure. Grace was amused at the way he kept glancing up at his car, just to check it was still there. In a very few minutes they were both behind their respective steering-wheels. 'I'm starting to pull now,' he shouted through the window. 'Try your engine as well.'

She did. Slowly, her car moved forward a foot or so then stopped. She heard her wheels skidding but then her car seemed to jerk forward, throwing her against the seat, and then bounced back onto the road. They had done it! She braked, got out of the car, and in the darkness made out him getting out of his.

'Thank you,' she said with real gratitude. 'That was very kind of you.'

He undid the tow-rope and smiled. 'I'm sure you'd have done the same for me.' Then he glanced at the nearest of her tyres and frowned. 'You do know these treads are very shallow?'

Of course she knew. But did he know how much four new tyres would cost? 'Yes, I'll be replacing them soon,' she said. She would have to. She didn't want any more shocks like today. She just wasn't sure where she was going to find the money.

'Wait a minute. You'd better not go until we've tested your steering and your brakes. You don't know what damage might have been done.'

'It's fine. The road from now on is straight and flat. I'll check both along there. Then I'll—'

'No arguments,' he said. 'I'm not that unreconstructed. Why don't I follow behind you just in case? Come on, would you leave me if the situation was reversed?'

Well, no, of course she wouldn't. And he had thought about it first, so he was a considerate man as well as a helpful one. 'Probably not,' she said, 'but I'm going all the way to Rivercut village. It'll take you miles out of your way.'

He laughed. 'It won't, you know. I'm headed there too.'

Grace stared. 'Then what are you doing on this road instead of the main route?'

'Funnily enough, I was asking myself that very question just before I came across you. My sat nav,' Mike added dryly, 'has a mind of its own.'

'Then I'm very grateful to it,' said Grace, recovering.

And, in fact, all did seem to be well. Her car steered without a problem, the brakes were good. She drove slowly, Mike following thirty or so yards behind. She suspected that if he thought she was going too fast, he wouldn't hesitate to let her know. He seemed to be a man who was perfectly polite, but who always made his point. Who on earth could he be visiting if he was heading for Rivercut?

The journey took perhaps half an hour and then they were in the outskirts of the village. Grace felt a rush of gladness, seeing the snow-capped roofs, the streetlights and the Christmas lights in the windows. As always, though, there was a pang as she passed the manor. She remembered previous Christmases with two great illuminated fir trees on either side of the front door and decorations in all the downstairs rooms. As a child she had found it wonderful. And she had thought it would last for ever.

Stop it, she told herself. You need to sell it, and you need to do it soon. You're living on fresh air once the mortgage has been paid every month as it is. Maybe a family would buy it, then it would have light filling it again. Light and love.

Fifty yards down from the manor entrance she drew up outside the small cottage that was now her home. Mike pulled in behind her. She stepped down from her car, grinning at the contrast between her old Land Rover and Mike's magnificent new machine. Ancient and modern!

Mike got out of his car too. With a smile she said to him, 'Thanks for the help. I hope I don't ever have to do the same for you. I'm not sure my vehicle would manage it.'

'Glad to be of service. There is one thing that occurred to me on the way. You had an accident as well as your car. You should really get yourself checked over. Now, I am a doctor…'

'Certainly not!' The very idea horrified her. 'I

am a nurse,' she pointed out. 'I can tell whether I'm injured or not.'

'If you're sure. Sometimes injuries aren't obvious at first.'

She knew that, but… She looked distractedly past him. And gasped. 'Something moved,' she whispered. 'Inside your car.'

Instantly Mike whirled away from her. She hurried after him as he opened the rear door and caught her breath again. There, safely cocooned in the back seat, was a child of about five or six years of age, just stirring into wakefulness. It was the last thing Grace had expected.

'It's all right, sweetheart,' said Mike softly, tucking the child's arm back under a cosy scarlet blanket. 'We're nearly at Grandad's house.' He glanced at Grace. 'My daughter, Bethany. It's not far to James Curtis's place from here is it?'

Grace knew her mouth was hanging open. Mike. Of course. She'd completely forgotten. Dr Curtis had said his son Michael was moving up here to join the practice. 'No, no, it's just along the main street and left by the green. I'm so sorry—I didn't realise who you were. No wonder you've got so much luggage in the back.'

She was babbling. Get a grip, Grace. And yet… She'd seen the front of his car quite clearly in her rear-view mirror. There hadn't been anyone in his passenger seat. She couldn't help looking again to make sure.

And his voice changed so suddenly that it shocked her. 'Correct. No wife, just my daughter.'

Had he read her mind? 'Well, you'd better get yourself and Bethany to Dr Curtis's house. He'll be waiting for you. I expect I'll see you at the surgery once you've settled in.'

'Not before you have your car checked over,' he said, unsmiling.

'Sure. Thanks again. Without you I'd have been properly stuck.'

As he got in his car, the light shone fully on his face. An unexpected thrill ran down Grace's spine. Dr Mike Curtis was a very handsome man. She didn't meet too many of them in the village.

CHAPTER TWO

THE cottage was cold. Grace hurried to turn on the gas fire before pulling the curtains. Then she went into the little adjoining kitchen and put on the kettle. She needed tea! She took off her coat, replaced her Wellingtons with furry slippers, and when the tea was made sank thankfully into her armchair in front of the fire. What she *should* be thinking about was how she was going to afford four new tyres. What she was actually thinking about was a deep, comforting voice and a thoughtful, considering presence. Mike.

How extraordinary that the man who had pulled her out of that wretched ditch had been the new doctor at Rivercut Practice! She tried to remember what she knew about him, but it was woefully little. James Curtis—her boss—was an open book himself, but reticent about his family. Mike had already been at medical school when

James had moved to Rivercut. He'd visited his father a couple of times. Now Grace came to think of it, she even remembered a wife and a baby at one point. And then—a year ago, had it been?— James had suddenly dropped everything and gone to London for his daughter-in-law's funeral. Everyone at the surgery had been shocked. They'd expressed inadequate sympathy when James had come back and said they hoped his son and the little girl were okay. Grace remembered James had said Mike was taking it hard.

She groaned. No wonder he'd sounded so bitter when she'd glanced at the empty passenger seat. Grace sipped her tea. They hadn't spoken much, but Mike had otherwise been friendly and good-humoured. It was part of a doctor's stock-in-trade to be approachable, of course, but even so Grace thought they'd be able to work together as colleagues without any of the awkwardness that sometimes took a while to settle down. And what's more, he'd fit in just fine in Rivercut. That lovely voice would have all the female patients eating out of his hand in no time.

Grace's toes were starting to thaw. She wriggled them, thinking how she really ought to keep a pair of winter socks in the car now that the weather had set fast. Even without today's accident, she'd been cold. And if Mike hadn't happened along, she'd have been frozen for sure, walking to the farm for help.

She smiled, remembering Mike's little girl snuggled up cosily in the back of his car. No wonder he'd kept glancing at it—not anxiety about the vehicle, as she'd thought, but concern for his daughter. Lucky Bethany to have such a caring father.

Grace sighed. Peter had been just as protective of her when she'd fallen pregnant. God save her, she'd been as foolish as her mother to be flattered by pretty words, chocolates and flowers. But Peter Cox's professions of undying love hadn't lasted beyond the moment when he'd caught sight of the probate papers and realised there was no money to go with the heavily mortgaged manor, and then her world had fallen apart yet again…

Mostly Grace was all right. She had her job, she had her friends, she had Rivercut. It was just that now and again—like when she saw a man tucking his small daughter's arm inside a cosy blanket—she missed her lost baby more than she would have believed possible.

It had been a long journey from London but, absurdly, Mike found himself slowing as he drove along the main street of Rivercut village from the church of St Lawrence, with its illuminated crib, to the green. It seemed like a festival of light. Every shop was decorated. Every house and cottage boasted at least one Christmas tree. Everyone here was making an effort. There was obviously a lot of local pride.

He'd seen very little of the village, only making a few short visits in the twelve years his father had worked here. With his busy lifestyle it had been simpler for his father to come to London. So there was no sense of coming home. Rather, a feeling of curiosity. What would it be like, living in a moderate-sized village rather than in London? Peaceful, he hoped. Certainly different. Dad had said there was a good community spirit in Rivercut, and Mike's brief encounter with Grace had definitely been an eye-opener. She'd shown no qualms at all at the prospect of knocking up the nearest farmhouse and asking for help. He still wasn't sure why he hadn't let her do just that, except that his masculine pride would have been stung—and she'd been right about that too.

He grinned wryly. If the truth were told, he'd been glad to follow her to Rivercut, not having quite the same faith in his sat nav as the salesman who'd sold it to him. He'd thought about Grace quite a bit as he had driven slowly behind her. He had only seen her in the half-light, but he'd had an impression of an above-average-height woman with what he suspected was a generous figure hidden by her fleece coat. He couldn't be sure about her hair—dark blonde, he thought, tied up in a pleat.

It wasn't her appearance that interested him most, though. It was her openness, her happiness with life despite having just skidded into a ditch, her apparent willingness to trust. Until right at the end, when she'd seen Bethany, and he could have sworn he'd seen a flash of something vulnerable under the cheerful, competent exterior. Had he imagined it?

Mike came to a halt outside his father's surgery and, as if on cue, from behind his seat there came the sound of his precious daughter waking up. Mike took a deep breath. It was time for them both to start their new life.

'Are we there yet, Daddy?' said Bethany sleepily.

'Just arrived, darling. Wait a minute, I'll come and unstrap you.' He undid the seat belt and lifted Bethany out of the car. She already had her coat on, but Mike pulled her woollen hat tight over her ears and wrapped the red blanket around her for good measure. They both regarded the surgery—a large Victorian house with an extension built out to one side. As well as the consulting rooms and pharmacy there was his father's flat where he and Bethany would stay until they found a place of their own. Bethany looked round, enchanted. 'It's been snowing,' she said.

The front door of the surgery flat was suddenly thrown open and a beaming James Curtis came out. 'Who's got a kiss for her grandfather?' he called. Bethany wriggled out of Mike's arms and ran through the snow towards the lit doorway. 'Grandad! We've come to live with you!'

She was growing up, Mike thought, left holding the discarded blanket. This was why they were moving up here. He looked at the delight on their faces, one young, one old. It would be all right.

Bethany's sleep had revived her. As Mike brought in the luggage, she ran from room to room, her dark curls bouncing, learning the layout, deciding where her toys would go and chattering nineteen to the dozen. Then she watched intently as Mike put her duvet and pillow on her new bed. She wore the same expression on her elfin face that her mother had always had when she'd been concentrating on a medical journal and, as always, it tore at Mike's heart. *Oh, Sarah.*

'She's very like her, isn't she?' said James in a low voice as Bethany ran in front of them towards the kitchen, just to prove that she knew the way. 'Must be a comfort.'

'Yes,' said Mike. 'Yes, it is.'

They had planned a special tea for this first night, Bethany's name written in alphabet spaghetti on a piece of toast. Then, of course, they had to write 'Daddy' and 'Grandad' and anything else they could think of too. Mike told his father it was a bit of a messy way of learning to spell, but he thought that it worked. Then came an even messier bath, with both Mike and Grandad ending up soaked. And last of all, after the teeth cleaning, it was her grandfather who was chosen to read her a bedtime story.

Much later, as they each nursed a glass of single malt in front of the fire, James said, 'It's a big change, Mike. From the heart of London to an isolated village on the Yorkshire moors. Are you going to manage?'

Mike shrugged. 'I think I will. The practice in London was growing faster than I wanted it to. I was doing more administration than medicine. I was too dependent on our friends for child care and…and everywhere I go in London I see Sarah. I need to get away. And I can do without the relentless social life that seems to be a necessary part of living there.'

'You might be surprised at the social life there is here,' his father warned with a grin. 'We don't all spend the winter sitting by the fire and watching TV. But I suppose you're right. It will be quieter here. And I told you there'd be fewer private patients. One or two—but not many.'

'I'll be glad to give them up. I don't need the money. I was paid a stupidly large amount when I was in the Middle East and I saved most of it. I've done well out of finally selling the flat and my partnership. I want to get back to basics. I want a quiet decent life for Bethany and myself, with more medicine than paperwork.'

'Seems a fair ambition. You know you'll be taking over most of the outside calls? There are plenty of them and we cover a large area here. I used to do most of them, but since I had that fall my doctor says I mustn't go out as much as I did.'

'Your doctor is?'

'Me,' said his father smugly.

'What about your partner? Can't she do them?'

'Rosemary? She's heavily pregnant. I don't want her going out any more than she needs to.'

'Well, I'll be happy to do as much travelling round as necessary. Provided my sat nav cooperates. Get some clean air into my lungs for a change.'

There was silence for a moment as James filled both their glasses. Then he said, gently, 'it's been almost exactly a year since Sarah was killed. How are you coping with it?'

Mike gave a short laugh. 'Mum died over twelve years ago. You still have her picture in your bedroom and I'll bet you think about her every night. How do you cope?'

'By remembering her and telling myself that she'd want me to be happy. And I am happy, most of the time.'

'Lucky you. I miss Sarah so much I ache. My friends seem to think I should be better by now, they keep trying to fix me up with suitable women. I've had a year dealing with a heartbroken little girl who'd lost the mother she doted on. That's taken all the emotional energy I've had to spare.'

'Ah, well. Grief has always had its own time-table. You might find you have more energy after you've spent a few months in Rivercut. Things are calmer here. Now, I'll just nip along to the kitchen and see how the casserole is coming on.'

Mike took another sip of his whisky, leaned back in his seat and sighed. Perhaps his father was right. Perhaps here he would find peace and contentment. Perhaps even an end to the night-mare that still came far too often—with a vision of his wife in the burnt-out wreck of her car.

No! He was starting a new life. He reached

resolutely for the leaflets and brochures his father had left on the coffee table, all with details of the property available locally. Staying with his father was all right for the moment, but he wanted a place of his own. He wanted a house with space and a garden. Somewhere Bethany could walk on her own down to school without him worrying about her as soon as she was out of sight. But as he turned page after page, his hopes fell. 'Nothing suitable for sale at all in the village?' he asked James when they were sitting down to lamb casserole and baked potatoes.

James shook his head. 'Not many people move out,' he said. 'And there's hardly any building allowed because we're in a national park. In fact, the only thing available here at the moment is Rivercut Manor. It belongs to my district nurse, Grace Fellowes.'

Mike looked at his father in amazement. 'Is she the only Grace in the area?'

'As far as I know,' said his father, mystified.

'Dad, I met a nurse called Grace on the way up. I pulled her car out of a ditch. A tatty Land Rover. But I left her at a cottage at the end of the village, not a manor house.'

His father sighed. 'It's a sad story. The wonder is that Grace keeps so cheerful all the time. Everyone feels sorry for her but she refuses to feel sorry for herself. Just keeps smiling and getting on with life.'

Mike was intrigued. 'So what happened?'

His father settled himself. 'The Fellowes family has been here for centuries. Once they owned most of Rivercut valley. Even seven years ago when Grace's father died, they were tolerably well off. They owned several local farms, they were good landlords. When Grace's father realised he was on his way out he sold the farms to the tenants. Grace was in the middle of her training and he knew his wife wouldn't be able to cope with rents and maintenance and all that. He put the money into two trust funds—one for his wife and one for Grace. Then a couple of years go by and Grace's mother takes up with a car dealer from Birmingham. Charming chap, squired her about, did the pretty. She fell for him in a big way, married him, signed every document he put in front of her, and then last year he did a runner to Spain, leaving the manor mortgaged to the hilt, the trust fund broken and Grace's ma without a penny to her name.'

'Oh, Lord. What happened?'

'Heart attack. Massive and merciful. But Grace still owes the bank a lot of money, she's barely clearing the mortgage payments and she has to sell the house to get straight.'

'And she's the Rivercut community practitioner?'

His father gave him an old-fashioned look. 'Up here she's the district nurse. She also does two or three clinics in the surgery for me. She's a brilliant nurse, knows everybody and everything. You'll enjoy working with her.'

'I think I will.' Mike was interested in this story. It suggested that Grace had a toughness that he had half suspected. He was looking forward to working with her.

As it happened, Grace was working in the surgery next morning. In theory she had appointments for wound management, injections and medical support for the first half of her clinic, then contraception, sexual advice and women's health. In practice, the receptionist fitted in people where she could. Grace enjoyed both sessions, even if the second one made her privy to rather more secrets than anyone else in the village suspected.

She had just finished giving a set of vaccinations to a couple who were going to Cuba for a long stay. Vaccinations against hepatitis A and B, typhoid, rabies, diphtheria and tuberculosis. She had given them the necessary brochures, but went through them herself so that they knew exactly what to expect. After the couple had left her consulting room, before the next patient was due, there was a tap on the door.

'Just grabbing a quick minute to introduce you to our new member of staff,' James said cheerfully. 'This is my son, Dr Michael Curtis, and his daughter, Bethany, who has a passion for knowing who works in which room and what goes on in all of them. I gather you've already met.'

'We have, and I've cause to be grateful.' Grace held out her hand. 'Good to meet you formally, Dr Curtis.'

He took her hand, shook it. 'Please, it's Mike. And it's good to meet you properly too. Dad tells me he's delegating all the home visits to me, so I expect I'll be working with you quite a lot. I'm looking forward to it.'

Last night had been an episode of torchlight and shadows; she'd hardly seen him clearly at all. But now was the bright light of day—and she had to admit that he was impressive. He was wearing a smart dark suit, a light blue shirt with some kind of college tie. He looked every inch the successful London doctor. Oh, dear, and yesterday she'd been covered all over in slush and mud.

To her embarrassment, he guessed what she was thinking. With a smile, he said, 'Bethany and I decided I should put on my interview suit because it's my first day, but in future I'll wear something more in line with the work I'll have to do.'

'In that case I advise clothes that are waterproof and easily cleaned,' she joked. Then she looked at the little girl holding her father's hand and smiled. 'Hello, Bethany, I'm Grace. You were asleep yesterday when your daddy's car pulled mine out of the ditch.'

Bethany's bright eyes darted about the room. They widened when they got to the photos on the shelf. 'That's a horse,' she said, and ran over to look closer.

Grace noticed the plastic pink horse clutched in Bethany's hand. She grinned. Was there a little girl alive without a pony fixation? 'She was called Sugar. She was my first pony. That's me riding her when I was a little girl.'

Bethany studied the photo. 'My teacher said I could ride a horse if I moved to the country.'

'I'm sure you will. There's a riding stable just outside the village where they have special classes for new riders.' Too late she saw Mike's muscles tense up. 'Once you've settled down, of course, and only if Daddy says you can.' And wouldn't the girls at the stable be all over him! Divested of last night's bulky coat, his body was trim—broad shouldered, narrow-waisted. Hair and eyes were both dark, his mouth well curved. Dr Mike Curtis was quite something.

'Yes, well, we've both got to find our feet first,' he said noncommittally.

Grace could read signals as well as the next woman and this one clearly said stay off the subject. James must have sensed it too. He suggested Bethany come and meet the receptionist and her daughter Rachel, who was off school with a sprained ankle. She'd seen the play area earlier, hadn't she? The little girl danced off happily. Grace and Mike were left alone.

As he looked at her she wondered if she could detect something in his eyes. Appreciation, perhaps, or even admiration? She had taken just a little extra care that morning. A little more attention to her hair, just a touch more make-up than usual. She didn't know why. Perhaps just to show a London sophisticate that not all country people were bumpkins with straw in their hair. Or to impress him? Whatever it was, it gave her a warm feeling when he looked at her with that searching expression.

'How's the car?' he asked.

Grace came back to earth with a bump. Fair enough. They *had* only just met after all. 'I took it into the garage first thing. Bert Machin said he'd have a look at it this afternoon.'

'You're not going to need it before tomorrow?'

'If necessary, I can borrow a car from Bert. I've done it before.'

He smiled. She liked his smile. It was starting to have the same effect on her that his voice did. 'The Rivercut spirit again, eh? I'd still be happier knowing that you—' But there was a knock on the door and a face appeared round it.

'Are you ready for me, Grace? You said… Ooh, sorry. Didn't know you had someone in here.'

'Wait outside a minute, Nina,' Grace said. 'I'll be right with you.'

Nina looked assessingly at Mike and then slowly disappeared.

'You've got work to do. I'd better go,' Mike said. 'I'll see you later, Grace.' And he too was gone.

The minute he was out of the door, Nina Carter rushed in. She was nineteen, a pretty girl who worked in a hairdressing salon in the next village and was the number one gossip in the area. A month ago, Grace had prescribed the contraceptive pill for her. Even after explaining patient confidentiality at some length, she'd still had to swear not to tell Nina's mother. And Nina had already said she wasn't going to use the practice pharmacy. She'd go into Whitby for it.

But now… 'Was that the new doctor, Grace?'

'Yes, young Dr Curtis.'

'He's fit, isn't he? Is he nice?'

'He's only just arrived. He seems to be a very practical doctor.'

'Is he married? Got a girlfriend?'

'Nina, I don't talk about doctors any more than I talk about patients. Now, you've been on the Pill for a month. Have you managed to take it regularly?'

'Yes. It's a bit of a job keeping it from Ma, but I've managed.'

'Have there been any unusual side effects? Headaches, mild depression?'

'No, nothing like that.'

'And you're still certain you want to go on with it?'

'Ooh, yes.' Nina grinned. 'Definitely.'

'Good.' Grace sighed. For a moment, she envied Nina her carefree attitude to relationships. It must save an awful lot of heartache. After ensuring that Nina was still practising safe sex, she dismissed her with a repeat prescription and welcomed in an older patient who was finding her unwelcome hot flushes rather hard to deal with.

It was a normal morning's work and she was enjoying it. But she couldn't get Mike out of her mind. What had James said last week? That his son could do with a whole new lifestyle? Mike was evidently going to be what she privately termed the 'outside man', doing all the driving to the outlying farms, so they would be working together quite a bit. She wondered if that would cause him any problems. She guessed he was four or five years older than her. They were both single. She could guess what conclusions the local gossips would draw. Oh, well, they'd soon find out they were wrong. Mike may be an attractive man, but the baleful memory of Peter Cox was still very much with Grace. She wasn't making new commitments any time soon.

Whilst talking to her patient, she rang through to James. 'I've just come across something, Dr Curtis, and if you've got a moment I'd like your advice.'

But it was Mike who walked in through the door, not his father. 'He says I'm to earn my keep,' he said with a smile.

That was fair enough, with the extra pressure they were under due to Rosemary Watson's unfortunate pre-eclampsia. Grace introduced Mike to Mrs Leaman, a fifty-five-year-old lady who had just started on HRT drugs to deal with her menopause. 'So far Mrs Leaman has benefited from the drug,' Grace said, 'but it seems to cause her the occasional headache in the morning.

She'll put up with it because in general she's feeling much better. But if it was possible to—'

Mike smiled at Mrs Leaman. 'I think HRT drugs are wonderful,' he said. 'They make life so much more pleasant. But let's see if we can get rid of the headaches too.' He looked at Grace. 'What did you prescribe?'

She told him and he nodded. 'A good choice. But since Mrs Leaman's having these headaches, how do you fancy trying something with slightly different proportions of oestrogen and progestin?'

He wrote down the name of a drug on her notepad. 'Perhaps we could try this?'

Grace looked at the name. 'It's new to me.'

'Not been out long. I can tell you more about it, though.'

They discussed the new drug with Mrs Leaman and Mike answered all her questions.

'So what do you think?'

Grace liked the way he asked her opinion, too. 'I think it's a good idea. Mrs Leaman, would you like to try this?'

'I certainly would. And thank you both.' The woman took her prescription and left.

'Mrs Leaman now thinks you're a wonderful

doctor,' Grace said. 'The news will be all over the village by the weekend.' Which had no doubt been James's intention. He could be a cunning soul at times.

'Does that mean that if I get something slightly wrong, it will be all over the village just as quickly?'

'You're catching on. This is an instant response environment. The Internet has nothing on Rivercut.'

'Going to have to keep on my toes,' he muttered. 'Actually, I'm quite looking forward to working with the same people over and over again. In London, a lot of my patients I only ever saw once or twice.'

'London has a larger floating population.'

'And some of them are sinking rapidly. I'm hoping that things will be a bit better up here.'

'Don't know about better,' Grace said, 'but probably different.'

'People seem more relaxed. In London everyone is in a hurry. There are things that they have to do.' He looked thoughtful for a moment and then added, 'Perhaps people aren't in a hurry here because there aren't so many things to do.'

'Ha! Just you wait. We don't want any of that fancy London talk in Rivercut. You'll be kept busy.'

It was fun talking to Mike. He had a sense of humour, wasn't going to take unimportant things seriously. Her phone rang. She picked it up. 'Yes, James, he's still here,' she said, and handed it to Mike.

Mike listened a minute, his face changing, then said, 'But what about Bethany…? Oh, okay, I'll be right there.'

He looked ruefully at Grace. 'Did you say I'd be kept busy? There's a small emergency and I'm to start work at once. I'll see you later.' And he was gone.

Grace had been right to think she would like working with Mike. She liked that his first thought had been for his daughter, not his own lost morning. As for anything else—and, yes, Grace admitted now that she was attracted to him—those sorts of thoughts were best banished. She'd made a huge fool of herself over Peter and she wasn't about to let herself in for any more hurt.

As Mike hurried to his father's room, stopping in Reception to tell Bethany he was going to be working for the rest of the morning and she was to be a good girl and play with Rachel where the other girl's mother could keep an eye on them, part of his mind was thinking about Grace. He was being perfectly detached about it. There was the same mild pleasure in thinking of her as he might feel watching a sunset or the snow on the hills. But, he had to admit, she was gorgeous. It wasn't just her height or figure, it wasn't even her dark blonde hair and clear complexion. It was her smile, her beautiful mouth, the way she was so happy with the world. And yet there was an alert look in her grey eyes that told him this woman was nobody's fool. He was going to enjoy working with her.

His first surgery. He hadn't expected to start work on his first day. He and Bethany were supposed to be settling in gently, meeting people gradually, looking for somewhere to live. But one of his father's long-term patients in the village had been suddenly taken ill, and James had offered to go round at once to see him. The other practice doctor being off with enforced bed-rest due to a sudden complication with her pregnancy, Mike had been volunteered to carry on with his father's morning list. This was not the kind of flexible arrangement that Mike would have expected in London, but he could see that it worked here.

So, his first Rivercut surgery and in his father's consulting room. A couple of suggestions that this was the room of an old-fashioned doctor—the panelled walls, the old roll-top bureau in the corner. It sat oddly with the computer on the desk and the printer under the window. Adjusting the swivel chair, Mike realised there were photographs on the wall opposite. A photo of his mother. A photo of him aged seventeen, covered in mud, racing down the pitch clutching a rugby ball. He smiled, remembering that game. And smiled more at the three photographs of Bethany. No wonder the receptionist had recognised her on sight.

Mike felt at home. He pressed the intercom to summon his first patient. Being new to the practice, he had to introduce himself to everyone, shake hands, explain that his father had been called away. And then there had to be a few words of general conversation.

He recognised what was happening after a while. He was being welcomed to the area. Yes, there was more snow here than in London. Yes, he had seen the poster inviting everyone to the Christmas carol service. Yes, his daughter would be going to the village school. No, he didn't think he would be lonely here.

His patients came in with the usual mixture of complaints, more minor than major. Gone suddenly deaf? A quick examination, then ear drops prescribed and come in to see the nurse in a week's time to have them syringed. A very bad cold? No, no point in antibiotics, they don't have any effect on a viral disease. Rest, plenty of fluids and paracetamol. A mole on the cheek that seemed to have grown over the past few weeks? Probably nothing, but we'll refer you to a consultant dermatologist at the local hospital—once he'd found out which one that was.

Then a case came in that was typical of the area. Dave Hart was clutching his back, obviously in pain. 'I was taking some feed out to the sheep, Doctor. I was loading up the trailer and I twisted a bit and suddenly there was this great pain in my back. Never felt anything like it.'

'OK, come and lie on this couch and I'll examine you.'

Sometimes Mike thought that the worst designed bit of the human body was the spine. He felt Dave's back, noticed where the pain was and observed what movement Dave had. 'Well, the good news is that I don't think that you've slipped any of the vertebrae. The bad news is you've strained the muscles quite badly. I'll prescribe painkillers, but the only real cure is rest.'

'Rest? Doctor, I'm a working farmer!'

'If you try to lift anything heavy, you'll only make things worse. Much worse. Isn't there anyone you can get in for a while?'

'I suppose so.'

Mike spent quite some time trying to make Dave see just how serious things could get if he did too much, but he had an uneasy feeling the man wouldn't know how to rest. And that would mean he'd be back.

His last case made him think too. Pip Lawrie, another young farmer, came in with a fungal infection of his feet, probably caused by getting them wet too often. 'The wife sent me,' he said sheepishly. 'Fed up with me itching all the time.'

Mike gave him advice and prescribed a spray that should clear up the condition. Then, just as he was leaving, Pip said, 'I don't suppose you can recommend something for a pain in the chest, can you? Just a mild pain.'

'You've got a pain in the chest?'

'Not me. Pa. He lives with us. He gets out of breath more than he used to and sometimes he complains about this pain. Says it's just down the front of his chest. It goes away when he sits down.'

Mike had a nasty feeling about these symptoms. 'I'd like to see him. Can he come down to the surgery?'

'Come all this way for a bit of a pain? No chance. No way will he leave the farm. He was born there and I don't think he's ever been more than fifty miles away from it in his life. He'll just carry on taking aspirin.'

'Not always the best thing,' Mike said cautiously.

'He's a tough old boy. You ask Nurse Fellowes. She used to come to the farm when he broke his arm.'

'Right,' said Mike.

It was lunchtime. Mike typed the last notes onto the computer, stretched, went into Reception to collect Bethany—and found the place empty! Where was she? Terror caught hold of him without warning. He flung open the front door but there was no one in sight. Really panicking now, he tore down the passage to Grace's room. 'Quickly,' he said. 'I need to—'

Grace looked up at him with a smile. Bethany also looked up from where she'd set up an improvised gymkhana on Grace's desk. 'Look at Twinkle, Daddy. He can jump right over the blood pressure machine.'

'Rachel had to go home,' said Grace, 'so Bethany's been keeping me company while you finished your list. My, but that Twinkle's an energetic little pony, isn't he?'

Mike just stood there, hanging on to the doorframe, feeling the adrenalin draining out of his limbs.

Grace's steady grey eyes rested on him for a moment. 'Tea, I think,' she murmured. 'Sit yourself down on my squashy chair with Bethany while I make it. Go and sit on your dad's knee, poppet.'

Bethany rushed across and threw herself into Mike's arms. 'Rachel goes riding,' she said. 'And Grace says she knows where. And—'

There was a knock at the door. James peered in. 'Where's the young lady who promised to have lunch with me?'

'Grandad!' Bethany leaped off Mike's knee, ran open-armed across the room. James winked at Grace and Mike. 'Just like her father used to be,' he said. 'Never walked when he could run.' Then the two of them were gone.

Grace put a cup of tea by Mike's elbow. 'I couldn't say I didn't know about the stables when she asked. Sorry if I've put my foot in it. Have you ever ridden?'

He shook his head. 'Once, when I was working in the desert, I was persuaded to go for a camel ride. I decided then that I was happier walking on two legs than being shaken about on four. I'll stick to walking.'

'Camels?' Grace grinned. 'I don't see you as Lawrence of Arabia.'

'Neither did the camel. Take a word of advice, Grace, stick to horses. They don't spit.'

'I'll remember that. Horses—good, camels—bad.'

He'd been feeling better until that moment, until an echo from the past seared across his brain, so painful that he gasped.

'Mike! Mike, are you all right? Your face has gone white. Are you going to faint?'

There was Grace in front of him, reaching out to him, her hands on his shoulders. Her smiling face was now concerned and he felt terrible for worrying her.

'I'm all right,' he managed to mumble. 'A bit tired. Yesterday was a long journey and…'

'Hush. Drink this tea, and I'm putting two spoonfuls of sugar in it. No arguments.'

He was in no condition to argue. He drank the sweet tea—which was disgusting—then felt angry at himself. He was a doctor, for goodness' sake. What had got into him? It was over now, done, finished. It had finished at ten p.m. on a wet November night when he had known at once what the news was. The A and E consultant had come out of Theatre and his face had told it all.

He would have to say something to Grace. He owed her that much for giving her such a fright. He'd make it short. 'My wife was killed in a car crash just over a year ago. I loved her very much but I've tried to put it behind me for Bethany's sake. Every now and again something brings the hurt back and it's…it's hard. You just said,

"Horses good—camels bad." What could be more harmless? Except that I remember Sarah saying it to me, those exact words. And we laughed about it.'

'Oh, poor Mike—I'm so sorry. So, so sorry.' He saw tears in her eyes. And then she was beside him, her arms wrapped round him, rocking him as his mother had done so many years before. 'So sorry,' she whispered again. 'So sorry...'

It was comforting, being held like that. He felt the tearing emptiness in his chest ease. But he was a man, not a child. He was a professional, a doctor. He didn't make an exhibition of himself. Reluctantly, he pulled away.

'It's me who should be sorry,' he said. 'I don't usually make a fool of myself like that. I—'

'You're not a fool! You were in love with someone who loved you and that is to be celebrated! And if you feel pain there is no shame in showing it. Right?'

'Right,' he said after a moment.

'I think that anyone who can love like that is...is wonderful. Wonderful and very lucky to have had it in their life. Would you like more tea before you go back to James and Bethany?'

'Please. But this time without sugar.'

He sat quietly sipping it, watching as she typed up her morning's notes. He found it comforting, he was glad he was with her. 'Thank you,' he said at last.

'No problem. I'd hazard a professional guess that you've been working too hard to grieve and have just bottled it up. You men are all the same.'

'Oh, that reminds me. Do you remember treating a man called Lawrie for a broken arm? About two years ago?'

Grace grinned. 'Joshua Lawrie. Lives with his son on High Scar farm. He's a cantankerous old so-and-so. Broke his arm in a farm accident—compound fracture, left radius—and it took twice as long to heal as it should have. He wouldn't stop working. I caught him trying to fork up hay one-handed. Why are you interested?'

'I've just had his son in. Apparently Joshua is complaining of chest pains, but he won't come down to the surgery.'

'I'm not surprised.' Grace looked at Mike. 'Are you worried about him?'

'It doesn't sound right. But I'm new here and don't want to be seen to interfere.'

'Well, I got on quite well with him in the end, so I could call in on them this afternoon and see how he's doing. Oh. No, I can't. My car's in the garage.' She bit her lip, then looked at him speculatively. 'You could drive me up there *because* my car's being fixed—then you could see him for yourself.'

'It's a good plan, but I promised Bethany we'd unpack this afternoon,' said Mike. 'I've neglected her all morning as it is. I wonder, though… I don't suppose you ever do calls in the evenings, do you?'

Grace laughed. 'Sorry. That really would put the wind up them. You're truly worried about this, aren't you?'

Mike shrugged. 'Occupational hazard. How about if we just say you're showing me the area? Bethany will be all right with Dad for the evening. I really would appreciate your assistance on this, Grace.'

She was silent for a moment. 'All right. About half past six?'

'That would be perfect. I'll see you then.'

Walking down the road to her cottage after Mike had gone, Grace thought of what she had just learned. His wife had been killed just over a year ago in a car accident. She'd known that already. What she hadn't known was that he was still in love with her. Grace was a trained nurse, she could read people, she had recognised the anguish on his face as being entirely honest.

So what did that mean to her?

Grace sighed. It meant she'd have to be careful. It meant that—whatever vague thoughts she might have been having about how nice he was, how attractive—she'd just have to give them all up. They would work together. They could even be friends. But nothing more.

Mike was in love with a ghost.

CHAPTER THREE

GIVEN that they were never going to be any more than friends, Grace was having a surprising amount of difficulty deciding what to wear. Not her uniform, that was certain. But did she dress as someone going out on a snowy winter's night—boots, trousers, thick sweater and anorak? Or did she dress more smartly? Like someone going out on a date?

Hmm. Mike's car was large, luxurious and capable of dealing with the worst conditions that there could be round here. So she would dress smartly. Not overdo it, but just make a bit of an effort. She started to run herself a bath. It would take time; the boiler was old and temperamental. Meanwhile, she went to her rather chilly bedroom and laid out three dresses on the bed. Which to wear? The dark blue lacy dress, the light blue wispy silky dress or the grey jersey dress with the swooping neckline?

Oh, for heaven's sake! She was going out to see a possible patient with a man she had only met yesterday. What was the point of dressing up? They were going to be *friends*. There was no need to impress Mike Curtis. She hung all the dresses back in the wardrobe and took out a pair of black trousers.

But she'd still look smart. She liked to look smart on occasion. In fact, when she had bathed and washed her hair, decided on a white silk shirt and a blue bolero jacket to go with the trousers and spent half an hour on her makeup, she decided she looked quite presentable.

To finish, a pair of black court shoes. Then she sighed and put her Wellingtons in a carrier bag. There would be the inevitable muddy walk between car and front door.

Mike was exactly on time and she felt a faint flutter in her stomach when she opened the front door to him. He was now in a black leather jacket and a dark sweater. There were snowflakes on his head and shoulders. He looked distinctly male, even more so than in his formal suit. In fact, he looked decidedly sexy.

'I'm ready,' she said, catching up her coat. 'Let's get straight off.' She didn't give him the option of coming into the cottage. For a start there was no need. And also this was in a sense her refuge, it was geared to *her*. If he came in he might feel to her like an intruder and she didn't want to think of him that way.

He didn't seem upset by any possible rebuff. 'Your carriage awaits you, madam,' he said.

She waved the carrier bag in front of him. '*Mesdames* in carriages don't carry Wellington boots with them to get through the mud.'

'If there was mud I would happily have carried you.'

Now, that was a thought that was rather exciting. But she said, 'We don't go in for a lot of carrying around here. Modern women make their own way, even if it's through mud. Come to that, they probably always did. Besides, your legs would buckle—I'm not exactly a stick-thin model.'

'I'm glad you're not,' he said, and she had to blush. But after she'd locked the door she didn't object when he took her arm to walk her through the snow.

Being driven in his Range Rover was infinitely preferable to driving her faithful old vehicle. It didn't rattle, it didn't smell of diesel, it didn't hesitate before climbing a hill. And the seats were so comfortable!

'I like your car,' she said.

'I think it's right for the job. The equivalent of my London Jaguar. I'm going to enjoy driving around here. I'm already getting used to the novelty of not stopping for traffic lights every hundred yards. Incidentally, what's the word on your car?'

'Very good. Nothing bent or broken. Bert's retuned the engine and done something incomprehensible with the carburetor. And he's getting me a set of re-moulds as soon as possible.'

'Re-moulds?' Mike's voice was sharp. 'Why not new tyres? You need them.'

'Bert says re-moulds will do the job.'

'They might do a job but not the best.'

Grace sighed. 'I can't afford new tyres. Re-moulds will be fine. It's hardly as if I'm going to do any racing. Getting from A to B is all I ask.'

'Point taken,' he said. He drove in silence for a moment. 'Just one thing—if this weather gets worse and you have to make a trip out to somewhere that's going to be really hard to get to, I'd like you to borrow this car.'

'What! Are you mad? This Range Rover costs something like double my annual salary!'

'It's insured. Tell me, Grace, if there was trouble and if I needed to borrow your car, you'd lend it to me, wouldn't you?'

'It's not the same.'

'How is it different?'

'It just is. You need to take the left fork here and keep going up. The road's a bit precipitous.' She pointed to a rack of CDs just below the dashboard. 'Shall I pick some soothing music?'

'Soothe away,' he said.

She needed to stop talking for a while. Mike was unsettling her. His offer to lend her his car— she could imagine some men making it solely to impress her. But she didn't think Mike was like that. It was a genuine, helpful offer and it only added to his attractiveness. Which, given the way he still felt about his dead wife, could be a real problem. Putting some music on would mean they didn't have to talk. It would keep things impersonal.

What was the last thing he had been listening to? She ejected the CD, looked at the title in the dim light from the dashboard and laughed out loud. '*Nursery Rhymes To Sing Along To?*'

He slanted a look at her. 'When we're bored with driving, Bethany and I sing duets. We're very good. Would you like to join me in a rendition of "*Ba Ba Black Sheep*"?'

'I think I'll pass.'

'We sing Christmas songs too. There's a CD of them in the rack. With finishing for the holidays so early, Bethany's been practising non-stop for her school Nativity since half-term, so we're pretty hot on carols.'

'That's handy. You'll be a big asset at the carol service. Talking of school…'

'She's booked into Rivercut Primary for January. I want her to grow up in the village.'

'That's good, but it wasn't what I was going to say. It occurred to me that the school here has still got a couple of weeks until the end of term. The reception teacher is a pal of mine—I'm sure she'd let Bethany start now if you wanted.'

'Well…'

'You know, Christmas is a great time for a kiddie to settle into a new class. It's all glitter and paper chains and snowflakes. And with you taking over Rosemary's list, it would mean Bethany is safe and occupied and happy while you're working.'

There was a silence as Mike negotiated two hairpin bends in succession. Grace held her breath. Had she said too much? Would he accuse her of interfering? 'You're right,' he said at last. 'I'll take her down there tomorrow and introduce ourselves.'

Phew, he hadn't taken her suggestion the wrong way. Grace riffled through the CDs with a feeling of relief. A lot were Bethany's but those he had picked for himself were a wide-ranging selection.

'You've got an interesting taste in music,' she commented.

'I have to give the non-musical answer. I know what I like.'

Grace slipped in a disc, but turned it down low. 'I like this,' she said. 'It's cheerful.'

Ten minutes later they drove into the courtyard of High Scar Farm. 'We were just passing,' said Mike with little regard for the truth. 'Nurse Fellowes is showing me the area and I thought we'd drop in. Mr Lawrie, this morning your son said that you'd been having some pains in your chest?'

'Indigestion,' growled Joshua Lawrie.

'Right. We can fix that—if it is indigestion. How have you been getting about in general?'

'All right.'

'No you haven't, Pa,' said his daughter-in-law. 'You've slowed right down and you know it. You can't get to the top of the stairs without catching your breath. And then these pains have started. Why indigestion now? You're eating the same food as you have for the past fifty years.'

'It's the sort of thing you expect when you get older.'

Grace looked at Joshua thoughtfully. She'd not seen him for quite a while, and it struck her that he had aged. He didn't move as smartly as he had done, his back was more bowed.

'Are you still forking the hay into the top loft, Mr Lawrie?' she asked. 'I remember how strong you were. You did it with just one arm.'

'Takes him all his time with two now,' said Pip. He got a malevolent look.

'Why don't we go into your bedroom and let me have a quick look at you?' Mike suggested. 'It'll only take a couple of minutes.'

'I don't see any point—'

His son interrupted. 'Go on, Pa. Doctor's come all this way to see you. It's only polite.' Evidently Pip didn't believe the story about the two of them just passing.

'All right, then.' It took quite an effort for Joshua to get up from his seat.

Mike followed him as they went upstairs. When they came down again, Grace could see that something had changed. Mike's expression was stern. Joshua looked half upset, half obstinate.

Mike stood in front of the fire. 'I've examined Mr Lawrie. What he's suffering from is not indigestion but angina pectoris. I think his blood vessels have narrowed, meaning his heart isn't getting enough blood. And this cold weather is only making things worse. I'd like him to go to hospital—and I'd like him to go now.'

'I'm not going to hospital! Not at this hour of night!'

'Pa! You've got to do what the doctor tells you. He's the expert.'

'I would like you in hospital tonight, Mr Lawrie. If you stay here, I know you'll go out in that farmyard tomorrow morning and the cold could kill you.'

'I was born here. I can die here.'

'No, Mr Lawrie.' All of them were silent. Mike's words had been said quietly but with considerable force. After a while he went on. 'Tell you what, I'll meet you halfway. You go to bed now, you stay in your own bed tonight, you wait indoors in the warm tomorrow morning until the ambulance comes for you. Okay?'

'I think that's very fair of the doctor,' Pip put in.

Seeing that everyone was ganging up on the old man, Grace added that the sooner he was in hospital, the quicker he'd be out. 'You might have an angioplasty or perhaps even a bypass operation, but it can be done in a day and afterwards you'll be well on the way back to the man you used to be.'

'All right,' growled Joshua, after a silence just long enough to indicate that he wasn't going to be a pushover. 'I'll be ready tomorrow.'

'Good,' said Mike. 'This is your chance to be both fitter and happier.'

The old man looked at Mike, then nodded imperceptibly. 'I'll go to bed now, then.'

They watched as he left the room. 'Nobody in the past fifteen years has been able to change his mind, Doctor,' said Pip. 'You're a miracle worker.'

'They'll work miracles for him in hospital,' said Mike.

'You achieved a miracle there,' Grace said as they travelled back down the snowy lanes. 'You managed to change his mind.'

'I knew if I insisted that he go to hospital tonight, and he didn't go, then he'd feel that he'd won a bit of a victory. He was entitled to that.'

'That's sneaky. You can be as persuasive as your father sometimes, can't you?'

'Perhaps.'

There was silence for a while. 'I'm starving,' he said suddenly. 'Have you eaten yet?'

'Cup of tea and a biscuit when I got in from work.'

'That's not enough. Is there a pub nearby where I could buy you a meal? We're both looking smart this evening and I think we deserve a treat after our successful visit.'

She looked at him assessingly. 'Just as colleagues?'

'Just that.'

'Then I'd love to,' she said lightly. Even so, she wouldn't choose anywhere too expensive. That would send out exactly the signal she wanted to avoid. 'I know the perfect place—providing you're prepared to be a little more flexible with your arteries than you are with Mr Lawrie's?'

'You're the navigator—direct away.'

'Well,' she said with a grin, 'the place is called The Hilltop for a reason…'

It was an excellent meal. They had a table in the wooden-beamed parlour, by the window so they could see the snow swirling around the moors outside. They had a bottle of good white wine. Fish fresh that morning from Whitby and the hotel's famous—or infamous—speciality: chips guaranteed deep-fried in pure beef dripping.

'I see what you meant about arteries,' said Mike. 'I don't think I'll ever eat another chip cooked in oil again. These are just heaven.'

For dessert, equally wonderful, they had rhubarb crumble and thick, home-made custard.

And then a cafetière of coffee. As she smelled the rich Brazilian coffee beans, Grace closed her eyes and smiled. 'Thank you, Mike. That was the best meal I've had in ages.'

'Likewise. We must come again. Soon.'

She opened her eyes in surprise. What did he mean, soon? She'd only known him for…was it really only twenty-four hours? But she reflected that in London he probably ate out with colleagues a lot. Networking. His offer wouldn't mean anything.

'So tell me about you,' he continued diffidently. 'My father told me you were having to sell the family home. Does it hurt to talk about it?'

His voice was gentle. Grace felt he genuinely cared. 'It all hurts, but it's something that has to be done. The mortgage payments are crippling. Did James tell you why?'

'He said your stepfather cheated your mother.'

'Cheated, but did it quite legally. There's no hope ever of getting the money back. Most of it has been lost in poor investments, from what I gather. I can't blame Mum. She was horribly lonely—and the man was a real charmer. I was happy for her—can you believe that? I hate men like him.'

'Not all men are the same.'

'So I thought. Until I found the man of my own dreams and it turned out that I was as big a fool as my mother. He was even more worthless than my stepfather.' She sighed. 'But I don't want to talk about Peter right now. I enjoyed the meal—and the evening—too much to want to be made angry.'

He reached across the table for a moment and gripped her hand. The physical contact warmed her, showed he understood. Grace was a tactile person. She understood how important touch was when used for comfort or silent sympathy. Mike's brief grip was judged just right and she appreciated it. But when he'd let go and was signalling to the waitress for the bill, she wished it could have gone on a bit longer.

As they walked down the hallway he paused by the illuminated Christmas tree. 'That's nice. I promised Bethany we could have a real tree this Christmas. Where do I buy a good one? The Forestry Commission?'

Grace shook her head. 'There's a plantation called Kilham's out on the Penthwaite road, it's not too far away. If you've got somewhere to plant it, get a tree in a special pot that you can put in the ground. Then you can keep it from year to year. But order one quickly, they soon disappear.'

'I'll do that.'

They walked out of the warmth of the pub into a moonlit wilderness. The snow had stopped, there was only the blanket of white over the peaks around them. Grace felt an uplifting excitement at the sheer beauty of it.

'Now, that's something you don't see in London,' said Mike softly. 'Truly magnificent.'

'I love it,' said Grace. 'It's so pure, so wonderful. It makes me think that everything just has to be all right really. Christmas will be white. Every child will get their favourite toy. People will laugh and be happy and…'

'You're an idealist, Grace.'

She grinned at him. 'Someone has to be.'

He cupped her elbow to steer her to the car. Did his hand take that bit longer to fall away?

As Mike started the Range Rover, feeling replete, he was shaken by a giant yawn.

Grace glanced across. 'Are you all right? Do you want to go back inside and have another coffee?'

He was touched at her quick concern. 'I'll be

fine. It's been a long day, that's all.' It had too. He let out the clutch and started back down the swooping road, mulling over the events. Beginning work two weeks before he was expecting to. The sense that the patients were comparing him with his father. The successful visit tonight. The hearty meal. No wonder he was tired.

'Yes, of course,' murmured Grace. She bent her head to search through the CDs and with a jump Mike knew she was thinking of his fright over Bethany's apparent disappearance that morning and that horrible, searing moment when he'd been reminded so vividly of Sarah.

'Don't you ever get furious?' he suddenly burst out. 'You lost your mother to a heart attack that could have been avoided. You were let down badly by someone you trusted. How can you be so calm all the time? So certain that the world is a good place? It isn't!'

Grace's head came up. 'Pull over,' she said.

'Don't be ridiculous. I'm driving you home.'

'Pull over,' she repeated. 'I want to show you something.'

There was a stopping place just ahead. Mike did as she asked.

'Come on,' she said. 'You can't see it properly from here.'

See what? But Mike followed her out of the car and across the road to where a bare-leafed tree stood sentinel on the wide verge of the ridge. The snow squeaked under their feet. 'Careful,' he muttered, taking her arm. She didn't pull away.

'What do you see?' she asked, nodding across the valley.

Mike looked. The village lay below the ridge: a crescent of snow-covered roofs and stained-glass curtains, all lit by the moon. 'I see Rivercut,' he said.

'Exactly. I did my training in Leeds. I enjoyed it—it's a nice city. But it's a *city*, Mike. When you look out of a top-floor window at night there are lights all around you—as far as the eye can see.'

Her breath made clouds in the frosty air. 'Meaning?' he asked, his breath mingling with hers.

She gestured below them. 'Look—it's like an illustration from one of those annuals I used to get every Christmas. I can see every house, every window. I can see the decorations. I can guess what's on the children's lists for Santa. It's… It's enclosed—and it's mine. I know them, Mike. I know every family. I look after them. And they look after me. It's what makes a person whole. It's what makes life good.' She looked up at him, her grey eyes clear in the moonlight. 'You're not convinced, are you?'

He was still holding her arm. Through the sleeve of her coat he could feel her warm, vital strength. 'I'd like to be,' he said. He sighed and tipped his head backwards, gazing up through a tracery of bare, snow-lined branches at the great silver disc of the full moon. Was Sarah up there? Watching over him now? Telling him to make a go of this new life?

Grace was still looking at the village. 'The Carters have put up even more lights. I'd hate to have their electricity bill.' But her face was gentle, not condemning. 'I do love Christmas,' she murmured. 'I know it's over-commercialised, but underneath there's still that hope, isn't there?' She glanced up. 'Oh! I can see a star in the east!' Then laughed. 'Except it's moving too fast and it's flashing.'

Mike laughed too. 'These aeroplanes get everywhere.' He continued to track the plane as it passed behind the tree. He frowned. There was a strange collection of twigs attached to one of the branches. 'What kind of bird makes a nest like that?' he said.

Grace turned her head to see. 'It isn't a nest. It's mistletoe.'

Mistletoe. Instantly there was a silence between them. He was aware of her breath on the night air, of her arm under his hand. The tension in her muscles told him she was just as aware of him.

He hesitated just a moment too long before he said, 'Mistletoe? I've never seen it growing wild like that.'

And Grace hesitated just a moment too long before she said, 'Well, there you go. You're in the countryside now.'

And neither of them looked at the mistletoe again as they headed back for the car.

CHAPTER FOUR

IN THE morning Grace had a number of calls to make in the village. Where it hadn't been swept, last night's new snow crunched under her feet as she walked from one house to another. The sun was shining, the snow sparkled and Christmas was most definitely in the air.

She came level with the school playground just as a barrage of shrieks announced the arrival of playtime.

'Hello, Grace!' shouted several of the children, tearing across with their coats open and their scarves flying. 'Where are you going?'

'I'm off to see a patient.' She smiled.

'Hello, Grace,' called another voice. It was Bethany, pink-cheeked and bright-eyed, holding hands with a new friend on each side.

Grace was pleased. She'd rung her friend Liz, the reception class teacher, last night, but she hadn't been sure Mike would actually take the plunge and bring Bethany down. 'Hello, poppet. Are you having a nice time?'

The little girl nodded enthusiastically. 'We made snowflakes and glittered them all over. I made one for you.'

'Thank you. I'll hang it up with my other decorations when I get them out. I hope you made some for Daddy and Grandad too.'

'I did. And Miss Lang says I can be in the Nativity!'

'That's lovely. Off you go and play now.'

Hmm. If Bethany was at school, Mike would be free after morning surgery. Thinking about a certain phone call she'd received earlier, Grace rang the practice.

'Grace? What's the matter? I can hear children screaming!'

'It's playtime, Mike.'

'Oh, sorry.'

Grace grinned. 'And before you ask, Bethany is building a snowman with a whole lot of new friends.'

'Has she got her coat on?'

'They've all got their coats on. She told me

she's been decorating snowflakes and she's going to be in the Nativity play.'

'She's *been* in a Nativity play. She was a king's page. You've no idea how much spin I had to put on to convince her it was superior to being an angel.'

Grace chuckled. 'The reason I'm ringing is to ask if you could drive me up to see a patient called Edith Holroyd this afternoon. She's a farmer's wife and is suffering from rheumatoid arthritis. I thought she was more or less stable but she phoned this morning asking if she could have a stronger dosage of drugs because the pain was coming back. I'm just a bit concerned. I'd like another opinion before she gets a fresh prescription.'

'It's what I'm here for—as long as I'm outside those school gates at three to pick up Bethany. And talking of picking up, you might like to know Pip Lawrie phoned to say Joshua grumbled his way into the ambulance which is even now heading for the hospital.'

'I know,' said Grace. 'I saw it coming through the village with Joshua's daughter-in-law driving behind to stop him escaping through the rear doors and doing a runner. I'll see you at the surgery after lunch, okay?'

'I'll be here.'

Mike found he was looking forward to doing another visit with Grace. He got a small rush of pleasure when she tapped on his door to ask if he was ready. She looked a typical district nurse with her neat uniform, tidy hair and minimal make-up, but there was a joyous inner core to her that in Mike's view made her a very superior community practitioner indeed.

As she directed him out of the village and up into the hills, he said, 'I had a look at Mrs Holroyd's notes—has anyone ever told you you write a fine report, by the way?—and I've signed out what extra medication might be needed from the pharmacy. It might save her or her husband a trek to the nearest chemist.'

'That's thoughtful,' said Grace.

Mike felt an absurd warmth at her praise. 'It's not something I'd have been likely to do in London, but it seemed obvious here. There is still the possibility that surgery might be necessary. Tell me more about her. What is she like as a person?'

'Sixty-three, daughter of a farmer, married another farmer who lived ten miles away. One daughter living locally, one son who emigrated to Australia and is farming a station out there that seems to be the size of Yorkshire. Never known any other life than farming and never wanted to. She can…she could…drive a tractor, shear a sheep, fork out feed. Only four years ago she could work in the fields for twelve hours and still turn out three hot meals a day for the family. Then she got rheumatoid arthritis and suddenly couldn't work at all. It's a tragedy! She hates just sitting around. Her husband loves her and wants her to be as comfortable as possible but he must miss the work she could do.'

Not a story you'd hear in London, Mike thought, but said nothing.

Grace continued. 'She knows that, barring some miracle cure, she's never going to get back to the person she was. She's never complained—but it grieves her. Life isn't fair sometimes.'

He was amused by her vehemence. 'Do you care for all your patients as much as this one?'

She shrugged. 'In this case, the family are friends. When I was a Guide my patrol used to go and sleep in their barn and Mrs Holroyd kept an eye on us. She used to accidentally cook too much dinner and need us to use it up for her.'

'She sounds like a good person.'

'She is. Her husband too.'

The farm was large and well kept. Mike didn't miss Grace's wistful expression as she glanced at one of the barns. Did she wish she was a young girl again?

Inside the farmhouse Fred Holroyd was on constant alert, fetching things for his wife, even though she scolded him and told him it wasn't necessary. Mike could feel the love between them. He liked Edith Holroyd too. He could tell the disease was sapping her strength, that she hated not being able to do the things that had once been so easy. He gave her a thorough examination—and sensed Grace's approval as she looked on—but he knew from the beginning that there was going to be no miracle cure.

He left Grace to help Edith get dressed and went back into the parlour. Fred was trying not to appear too hopeful. Mike examined the pictures on the wall while they waited. Most of them were photographs—some obviously of children or grandchildren but others were much older. Pictures of a kind of farming that had now disappeared.

When Grace and Edith came in, he said, 'Mrs Holroyd, I'm going to alter your medication. It should make your life a little easier, help you to sleep better. But you know this is in no way a cure.'

'I know. I've accepted that. There's worse off than me.' There was toughness in the voice but also just a thread of desperation.

'What do you do to occupy your time?'

'I cook still. I read. It's nice to have the time, now I'm not in the fields any more. I like it when my grandchildren come round. Helen brings them at least once a week. And I write to my son in Australia.'

Mike nodded, an idea forming. 'You must have seen a lot of changes. I've been looking at your photographs—some of the farming scenes date back to your childhood.'

A small smile creased Edith's face. 'I was helping in the yard when I was six,' she said. 'Not getting in the way, mind, but helping. My father paid me—he gave me a shilling and some sweets.'

'Ever thought of writing down your memories?

To pass them on to your children and grandchildren?'

Mrs Holroyd looked shocked. 'Me! I couldn't write!'

'You write to your son. Just think of it as a series of letters. Start by listing all the jobs you did in the yard. It's a fast-disappearing way of life. People will be interested in the years to come.'

'I think that's a great idea,' said Fred. 'You always tell a good story, Edith.'

'Well, I've got some memories,' she admitted. 'I'll give it a go.'

'You're an odd sort of doctor,' said Grace as they crossed the farmyard to the car. 'I'm really impressed. That idea you gave Mrs Holroyd—that she write out her life story—that was inspired. It'll probably do her as much good as the medicine.'

'Just so long as she keeps taking the medicine! But thanks—one of the reasons I wanted to come up here to Yorkshire was that I thought there might be the chance to spend more time talking to patients. Not the ten minutes allocated to them in the surgery but an opportunity to get to know them.'

'In an ideal world,' Grace said. She opened the passenger door, then paused. 'Can you hang on a moment? There's something I need to collect. I won't be long.' And she walked quickly over to the barn she had looked at before.

Mike watched, surprised, as she pushed open the unlocked door. She obviously knew what she was doing, but even so…

It wasn't a barn for agricultural use. He'd been on City Farm excursions with Bethany and this building didn't have anything like the requisite dusty, cobwebby atmosphere. Or the smell, for that matter. As Mike stepped through the doorway his eyes took in a new concrete floor, a sound roof and solid walls. There were packing cases stacked along one wall and furniture, wrapped in thick insulating sheets, at the far end.

Grace was rummaging through a packing case, lifting out cardboard boxes.

'I assume the Holroyds don't mind you making off with the crown jewels, do they?'

She didn't look round. 'It's not the crown jewels and they know all about it. Please, Mike, just wait in the car. I really won't be a moment.'

He was startled. Her voice was ragged with tension. 'Can I help you carry anything?'

'It's fine. The boxes are very light. Please, Mike.'

He put his hand on her arm, just for a second. 'No hurry.' But it was a puzzle—the first time he'd heard her sounding less than in control. It made him feel... He didn't know how he felt. So once they were in the car heading for Rivercut again, boxes safely stowed in the back, he started talking about the government's latest plans for reorganisation of the health service. It wasn't exciting, but it was something that concerned them both, and on which they both had views. A sensible talk between two professionals. He was sure they both benefited from it.

When he drew up outside Grace's cottage, she unloaded her three cardboard boxes—they really were light, he noted with interest—looked at her watch and said, 'Ten minutes for you to get to school. Perfect timing.'

He glanced across at the side road leading down to the school. It wasn't exactly solid with cars, but enough to make parking interesting. 'I couldn't leave the car here while I collect

Bethany, could I? Save doing a turn in the road in the snow with everyone watching.'

She raised her eyebrows. 'Says the man who used to drive a Jaguar in London. Yes, of course you can. Go on, you don't want to be late.'

'Thanks. Well, see you tomorrow, I expect.'

Grace shut the door behind Mike and let out a breath she hadn't realised she'd been holding. Her gaze fell on the boxes of Christmas decorations the Holroyds had been storing for her. Ridiculous to get so upset. She gave a mighty sniff and went to put the kettle on for a comforting mug of tea.

But the kettle had only just boiled when there was a knock on the door. On the doorstep stood Mike, a beaming Bethany—and a very, very glittery snowflake.

'She made it for you,' said Mike with a perfectly straight face. 'So I knew you'd want it right away.'

'Thank you, poppet. It's lovely,' said Grace. A small shower of silver transferred itself to her uniform cardigan as she took the star.

'Yes, it is,' agreed Bethany. She gave an excited skip. 'I'm going to be an angel!'

Some spin, thought Grace, looking at Mike.

He looked back. 'And, um, she has to have a costume as soon as possible. Tomorrow, for preference. I asked about hiring one. Everyone fell about laughing. The teacher thought you might be able to help.'

Oh, did she? Grace was going to have words with Liz next time she saw her. 'Well, all you need is a white pillowcase and a couple of lengths of tinsel, but… Wait a minute…' She'd remembered something. 'Actually,' she said slowly, 'I do have an angel costume ready made. It used to be mine. But it's at the manor. In the attics.' And that would mean going back there.

'That would be great. Can we take you? Bethany and I? In the car?' said Mike, and then he saw her expression. 'But, of course, I understand if…'

Grace shook herself. It was just a house and an attic and a box of dressing-up clothes. She smiled at Bethany. 'I'll fetch the keys.'

The manor stood on rising ground just outside the village. No one had been up the drive for quite a while, so the snow lay thick along it. The afternoon sun gilded the mellow Georgian facade and there were flashes of light reflected from the icicles hanging from the eves. Grace hadn't expected this to hurt quite so much.

Bethany was clamouring to get out as soon as Mike stopped the car.

'It's beautiful,' he said quietly. 'Like an illustration out of one of Bethany's fairy stories.'

But without the prince, thought Grace. She unlocked the double outer doors, then the inner doors. There was a film of dust everywhere—and it was cold. But that was why she'd moved out. It took too long and cost too much to heat. She simply hadn't been able to manage it by herself.

Mike followed her in. 'No furniture?' he queried.

'The agent advised it. He said the corporate bods prefer to see floor space if they're thinking of out-of-town headquarters.' But it was horrible, hearing their echoing footsteps where once the sound would have been absorbed by sofas and bookcases and low tables and colourful rugs. She tried to see the empty hall through Mike's eyes. An elegant oak-panelled room, built in the days when the hall had been the main room of the house. An ornate fireplace, now blocked up against the draughts from the chimney. A graceful staircase leading to an open landing.

Bethany gave a squeal of delight and ran past them to start climbing the stairs. Grace gave a shaky smile. 'We used to have parties in this room. You should have seen it—they were glorious. And beforehand I'd borrow one of my mother's long skirts and walk down the stairs, holding my dress just above my ankles and feeling beautiful. Exactly like the actresses in the films Mum loved watching.'

'I imagine you outshone them all. Bethany, sweetheart, be careful on the stairs.'

'They're shallow, Mike. It's quite difficult to hurt yourself falling down them.'

But he was hurrying up after his daughter, so Grace followed.

On the landing, Bethany demanded to know what was in all the rooms. 'Sorry,' said Mike. 'It's a passion of hers.'

Grace would have preferred to collect the dressing-up box and go, but she couldn't disappoint that bright, excited little face. 'This used to be my bedroom,' she said.

It wasn't too bad, coming in here. She saw

Mike look around, noting the brighter patches of wallpaper where her wardrobe, bed, chest of drawers and dressing table had stood. Bethany ran to the window to look out.

'My desk was under that window. When I was tired of studying, I could stare at the moors. Probably why I love them so much.'

'I'm trying to imagine you as a schoolgirl. What were you like?'

'Gawky,' she said, and Mike smiled. 'With pigtails. That wall was covered with pictures of pop stars and horses. Dad always said the horses were better looking. You've got all that to come with Bethany.'

She led them down the passage towards the attic staircase. But Bethany reached up to open the next door along. 'Daddy!' she gasped, looking in. 'It's a princess bed!'

'Ah,' said Grace. 'That was my parents' room. The bed was built actually in there goodness knows how many generations ago. The only way to get it out would have been in pieces, so I left it for the time being.' Peter had talked grandly about knocking through the wall when they were married and turning her room into a palatial en suite. She wished she'd known before she'd got engaged how much of his love had had its roots in pure, unadulterated snobbery.

'It's a hit with one little girl, that's for sure,' said Mike. 'Sweetheart, don't bounce up and down on the mattress like that. It's ever so dusty.'

Grace was glad to be distracted from her memories. 'Bethany's not asthmatic, is she?'

'No, I just...' He broke off. 'It's a lovely light room too, with these windows on two sides. Views of the whole valley.'

'Yes.' Peter had loved that too. The fact that up here he had been lord of all he'd surveyed. Suddenly Grace wanted to retch. 'The attic is this way,' she said abruptly. 'You'll like this, Bethany. There's a cupboard door—and when you open it you find a staircase instead.'

Mike's daughter immediately bounced off the bed and raced past Grace round the corner to open the next door. Except that wasn't the attic staircase. Grace stood rooted to the spot, the desire to be sick even stronger.

Mike brushed past. 'Bethany, wait for me before you start climbing...' He looked into the room, stood perfectly still for a second, then shut the door gently. 'Not that one, darling. Let's try the next. Wow! Stairs! Just as Grace said. Carefully now.'

Feeling came back to Grace's nerve-ends. She followed them up the enclosed staircase, smiled wanly as Bethany ran in and out of the little attic bedrooms, unlocked the end room she'd been using for storage. Then she retrieved the box with the angel costume in, and went downstairs.

'Sorry,' said Mike again. 'She's going to want to look everywhere on the ground floor too. I swear she's going to be an estate agent when she grows up. It's hurting you, isn't it, showing someone around your home?'

'I've had easier tasks,' said Grace.

'You don't do it when someone is interested in buying it, do you?'

'No, I leave it to the agent. I couldn't bear to see their faces as they look at the shabby wallpaper and the old Victorian toilet fittings. Any big company would gut the place and refit it anyway.'

'You love it very much.'

'Of course I do. It's my home. Mike, do you mind if I wait outside while Bethany looks at the downstairs rooms?'

'We'll be quick.' He put his hand on her shoulder, gently. She reached up, touched his hand and then moved to the door.

She had time to regain her equilibrium before they joined her. It was ridiculous to get so worked up. The manor had to be sold and that was an end to it. She locked the doors and turned to see that Bethany, like all children everywhere, had been unable to resist the lure of the wide sweep of untouched snow in the orchard to one side of the drive.

'Not too far, sweetheart,' called Mike, an edge to his voice. 'It's getting dark and I don't know how deep it is.'

Grace looked at him curiously. Surely even in London there were places where a child could fall full length in the snow with perfect safety? How on earth did he think snow angels were made? 'Let's run and catch her,' she suggested. 'I used to love it when my parents did that.'

He cast her a swift, grateful glance and pelted one way. Grace ran the other way in a pincer movement. Bethany shrieked happily and did indeed fall full length in the snow, suffering no ill effects at all.

She let her father scoop her up. 'What's that?' she said, pointing up into the branches of the nearest apple tree.

'Mistletoe,' said Mike knowledgeably. 'People kiss under it.' And he kissed his daughter on the forehead.

Bethany was charmed. 'Grace kiss me now,' she demanded.

So Mike put her down and Grace bent to give the little girl a hug and a kiss.

'Now Grace and Daddy.'

There was a tiny silence. Grace straightened up. Her eyes met Mike's.

'Absolutely,' said Mike. He put one hand on her upper arm and moved forward. Just the most delicate touch of lips on lips. They were cold, but a thrill passed through Grace that she had never quite felt before. She rested one hand on his body, felt the fast beating of his heart through his coat and leaned forward. He kissed her again, warmer, slightly longer, but just as soft. 'For luck,' he said. Then let out a breath, hoisted his daughter up to his shoulder and walked back to the car.

CHAPTER FIVE

TEA was over. Bethany was having a bedtime story read by Grandad. There was no evening surgery—and Mike was walking down Rivercut High Street to Grace's cottage. She'd noticed some places where the tinsel trim needed to be sewn back onto the angel dress. She'd take it straight over to the school tomorrow. No need, he'd said, I'll come down later to pick it up.

Which he was. Wondering at himself the whole way. That kiss. Just a friendly peck he'd meant it as. But the moment their lips had touched it had ceased to be a friendly gesture and had *meant* something. Trouble was, he didn't know what. And with Sarah an ever-present ache in his mind, if the kiss had meant something to Grace too, he'd have to break off whatever it was. It wasn't fair to her. But it had been lovely. And— yes, he admitted it—too short.

'Hi,' said Grace when he knocked at her door. She'd changed into jeans and a jumper and let her hair down. It was longer than he'd thought, and very attractive. 'Come in—and before you say anything, yes, it is a bit of a contrast to the manor.'

Mike smiled. 'On the contrary, you've made a tiny space look quite large.'

'Thank you. Mrs Johnson up the road remembers families of eight or nine children living in these cottages. Personally I think it does just nicely for one—like a comfortable set of clothes that I put on when I enter the front door.'

'I shouldn't gain any weight, then,' he said with a grin.

'I can't, I'm too busy. I've got the angel costume for you. Oh, and I found my photo albums for Bethany so she can see what the manor looked like with furniture in. You're welcome to borrow them.'

It was a clear hint but, 'I don't need to rush home straight away,' he said.

'That's a pity,' said Grace.

He laughed out loud at her honesty. 'And that's why. I think we might need a small talk, don't you?'

'I suppose so. I'll make some coffee. Sit on the couch—you won't loom as much.'

But he didn't sit. He wandered around the room. It wasn't very warm. Did she not notice? Or was she really too hard up to heat it properly? He turned to see her watching him from the door to the kitchen, an anxious look on her face. 'This is a handsome sideboard,' he said, stroking the polished walnut surface.

'It's Georgian. Practically the smallest piece of furniture from the manor.' Then she hesitated. 'You've probably guessed what was stored in Mr Holroyd's barn was the rest.'

'I wondered.'

'I know I need the cash, but I just couldn't bring myself to sell everything I'd grown up with. And if I get somewhere larger to live then I'd like to keep a few more pieces.'

'Seems a good idea. What was in the boxes you brought back today?'

She grinned. 'Christmas decorations. I realised when Bethany told me about the snow-flakes this morning that I hadn't put mine up yet.' She ducked back into the kitchen and re-appeared with two mugs of coffee. She handed him one then sat cross-legged on a large cushion by the wall.

Mike felt the tiniest bit impatient. 'Oh, come on, Grace. This might be a small couch, but there's plenty of room for two.'

She waved him to sit down. 'I sit here a lot. Good for the posture.'

'Really? Your posture looks pretty good to me.'

'Shows it works.' She reached under the coffee table for a couple of albums. 'Here,' she said, passing them to him. 'The manor.'

'Grace, this is silly. Come over here and show me them properly. I don't bite.'

'It's not biting I'm worried about.'

Mike's gut clenched. 'And *that's* what we need to talk about. Grace…'

Her mobile rang, making him jump. 'Sorry,' she said. 'The trouble with having been born in Rivercut is that people don't always realise I have off-duty hours.'

But it wasn't someone needing medical attention. And the moment Grace said 'Hi, Bert. The car's ready? That's great! How much do I owe you?' Mike suspected he ought to be leaving.

He downed his coffee double quick, burning

his throat, grabbed the bag with the angel costume in and had nearly made it to the door when Grace put out a hand, barring his way.

'I don't quite understand, Bert. Why is there no charge for the tyres?'

'I'd better go. Bethany will be—'

She toggled the mute button. 'You're in no hurry, remember? Yes, Bert, I understand they're fantastic tyres and will probably outlive the car, but how much did they cost?'

Mike winced.

'*How much?* Six hundred pounds? That's three times the… Pardon? Dr Curtis said the practice would pay? Yes, wasn't it nice of them? Yes, it was a surprise to me too. Refresh my memory, Bert. Would that be old Dr Curtis or the young one?'

She listened for a moment more and rang off.

Get in first, thought Mike. 'No arguments, Grace. You use your vehicle to work for the practice and it just wouldn't have been safe enough with remoulds. You are no good to us or to your patients if you break down.'

'You pay me for using my car! I claim every inch of mileage I'm entitled to.'

'Forty pence a mile doesn't come anywhere

near covering your usage. The cost of those tyres is worth it to me because I now know that you're safer in bad weather than you were.'

'I thought you said the practice paid.'

'Me, the practice—what does it matter?'

'It matters because I have to know who to pay back!'

'Nobody!' He bit out his words in frustration. 'You weren't safe in that car and I'm not having anybody else I care about die in cars when I can do something about it!'

He didn't realise he had a look of anguish on his face until Grace put her hand up to his cheek. 'Mike?'

He stumbled back to the sofa and put his head in his hands. 'Leave me alone.'

He felt the sofa dip. 'Not a chance.'

'Okay, then. You've been warned. This isn't pretty.' He took an immense breath. 'Sarah—my wife—worked with me in the practice. She was a good GP—better than me. Neither of us were supposed to be on duty that night, but Sarah got an emergency call from one of her patients and felt she had to go. It was raining, the roads were slippery, she was in the little runabout, not the

Jaguar.' He took another deep, shuddering breath, conscious of Grace's arm around his shoulders but seeing only the slick, wet tarmac and the blazing lights of the traffic. 'It wasn't her fault, the inquest decided that. A lorry coming the other way swerved to avoid a car pulling out of a side road and lost control. Sarah braked, she had lightning reflexes, but she skidded and the lorry smashed into her. It almost flattened the little car and it caught fire. She died in A and E.'

Now both her arms were around him. 'Oh, Mike. Oh, Mike.'

He turned instinctively, buried his head in her shoulder, curling into himself with the pain of the memories. 'I looked at the police report afterwards, got to talk to the mechanic who had examined the wreckage of the car. He told me the tyre treads were within the legal limits. But if there had been just a little more tread then she might have stopped just a few feet sooner, might not have skidded. I was the one who saw to the maintenance of the cars. I can't forgive myself for that.'

Grace was crying too. Mike felt her tears splash against his forehead. 'You weren't to blame for the accident!'

'But I'm to blame that Sarah died.' He pulled away. 'I'd better go.'

'Not like that, you won't. I'll make some more coffee.'

He leant back against the cushions, drained. But in a strange, horrible way he felt better. He'd never said it out loud to anyone before, that he knew he was to blame for Sarah's death. Grace returned, sat down next to him and put a warm mug between his hands.

'Drink,' she said. 'It'll do you good.'

More silence. He sipped the coffee, felt its warmth trickle into him. For want of anything better to do he opened one of the albums. 'The manor,' he said. 'All dressed up for Christmas.' To be accurate, it was the manor at night. All the windows were lit, swags of coloured lights had been fixed to the elegant facade and there were two large Christmas trees, one either side of the front door.

Grace smiled. 'Those trees are still at the back of the hall. They're quite a bit bigger than that now. We used to enlist the regulars at the pub each year to heft them into place. Lots of people have said it doesn't seem the same without them this year.'

Mike turned the pages. 'Oh, wow,' he said at a photograph of the entrance hall set out for a party. A party in the grand style too. 'I see what you mean about it looking splendid. You ate like this every night?'

'Idiot,' replied Grace.

The hall was decorated and there was a huge Christmas tree next to the fireplace with presents piled underneath. Tables had been arranged in the form of a big T and covered in white cloths. Arranged on them was a vast buffet. And frozen in time were the smiling guests. Mike could almost hear the chink of glasses and buzz of good-humoured conversation. It could have been an old-fashioned Christmas-card scene of the squire and his guests making merry—but brought up to date.

He realised that Grace was leaning against him. She seemed to be doing it quite uncon-sciously, a woman who was used to touching, who wasn't uncomfortable with herself. 'Now do you see why I like Christmas so much?' she said. 'Everyone looks so happy. As if they think this can go on for ever. I wish the manor looked like that now, instead of horrid and echoing. Look, there I am! Holding my mother's hand.'

Mike bent to look closer. Grace's hair brushed his cheek for a moment. Yes, he could see her now. A young Grace, about ten years old. Her hair had been a lighter blonde then, but she radiated the same inner joy. 'And with a smart long dress,' he said, trying to sound prosaic. 'Is that the skirt you borrowed?'

She chuckled. 'No, it's a real dress—sort of. I threw a tantrum because I didn't have anything long to wear. Everyone else was in a full-length dress, why not me? So my mother fashioned that dress out of a real Indian silk scarf. Took her half an hour. I thought I was the best-dressed woman in the place.'

At which point Grace did notice that she was leaning against him. She got up hurriedly. 'There are photos of the other rooms there too. The music room, the dining room, my father's den. Take them to show Bethany.'

Mike stood reluctantly. It had been nice, sitting there with Grace. 'I will. She'll be fascinated.'

Grace moistened her lips. 'Mike—I do need to repay you for the tyres somehow. If you've ever been…quite well-to-do and then find yourself quite definitely poor, then you get very edgy if you think you're being offered charity. And before you say anything, I know at times people offer things and you should accept them in the spirit they're meant, but it's not so easy when you've only met that person three days before.'

He sighed. 'Without boasting,' he said, 'a large sum of money to you is not so large to me. For various reasons I'm…well, comfortable. It pleases me that people should be able to share in my good fortune.'

'Maybe so. But I'm not very good at being indebted.'

'You could help us integrate with the village, if you like. You know everyone and we know no one.'

'Except your dad, who *does* know everyone,' she murmured.

'I want Bethany to be settled here. Part of the community.'

Grace laughed. 'She'll do that without any help from me. I've never met such a friendly child.'

'Tell me about it,' muttered Mike. 'Do you know how many sleepless nights that friendliness gives a father?'

'She'll be fine. Now she's at school she'll be invited to tea and to parties. She'll go swimming and riding with the other kids. She'll… Now what's the matter?'

'Nothing.' And it was nothing. He would have to get over this protectiveness. And he may as well start now. 'There is one thing,' he said slowly. 'She wants to ride. Will you take her for me?'

Grace looked puzzled. 'The beginners' class is in the afternoon straight after school. You could take her yourself.'

'No, I can't,' he ground out. 'Horses are large and dangerous. Bethany is small and infinitely precious. If I take her, I'll be up there on the horse's back with her. Probably not very clever in the street-cred stakes.'

'Mike, the instructors are trained. This is their livelihood. Why would they teach kids something dangerous?'

Suddenly he needed to be out of this small room. He needed air to breathe and space around him. 'I have as much right to be irrational about my only daughter as the next man,' he said. 'But, equally, I don't want to infect Bethany with my prejudices. Just make the arrangements and stay with her the whole time, will you? Please, Grace?'

She opened the door for him. 'I'll give the stable a ring. She will be safe, Mike.'

'Good,' he said. 'Good.' And strode up the high street through the cold, crunchy snow, feeling as if he was about to throw up.

Thursday morning. Grace did her early calls, then went to the surgery to write up her notes and get ready for her diabetes clinic. After last night's emotional exchanges she had thought long and hard about how to behave around Mike and had decided it would be best for both of them if she adopted the same cheerful camaraderie with him as she did with his father. As for that kiss yesterday afternoon (over which she had expended even more long, hard thought), that had been so fleeting, such a nearly precious moment, that she wasn't going to let any highly charged personal stuff get in the way. Truth to tell, she wasn't sure yet how she felt about Mike. The pull of attraction was there—on both sides, she thought—but she didn't think he was ready to love another woman yet, and she couldn't see herself trusting another man with her heart for a long time to come.

Accordingly, when Mike put his head round the door and asked if she minded him sitting in on her clinic, she said, 'Yes, I do mind. Go and play with your own patients.'

It was evidently the right tack. He moved a chair to the corner of the room, unperturbed. 'My list this morning seems to be composed entirely of young women who have come down with mysterious colds or unidentifiable aches. I've shifted them to Dad and the nurse.'

Grace grinned. 'Well, you can't blame them. You're novelty value.' *And great eye-candy.*

'That's what Dad said.'

'Okay, you may observe my clinic with pleasure—not that it would make any difference if I did object, I suspect—but first I've got bad news for you. Bethany can start her riding lessons today. For now she just needs a pair of jeans, a jumper and a loose coat. I can take them home with me, get her changed at my place, and then drive her to the stables. It's a couple of miles past the manor.'

Mike didn't look thrilled, but said he'd get the clothes out.

Grace's first patient was Angela Mather, a busy

mum who nodded approvingly as Grace explained to Mike that Angela had had type 1 diabetes from an early age, managed it herself with insulin injections and was here for her annual check-up.

'I saw you yesterday at school,' she said while Grace was checking her blood pressure and taking a blood sample. 'My Joanne was telling me all about your Bethany. Played together all lunchtime, she said. Would she like to come to tea one day? Oh, and you must bring her to the Rivercut children's Christmas party next week. I'll put you down for sausage rolls, shall I?' She rolled down her sleeve, nodded when Grace said she'd be in touch about the results, and hurried off.

'Children's Christmas party?' said Mike faintly.

'In the village hall next to St Lawrence's. I'll do you a check-list.'

Her next patient, Mr Dobbs, told Mike at length that North Yorkshire had a 98.9 per cent record of good diabetes health care as opposed to the national average of 98 per cent. Grace didn't dare meet Mike's eyes as she relayed the information that Mr Dobbs was a newly diagnosed type 2 who needed regular monitoring and had never missed an appointment yet.

'Good grief, he knew more about diabetes than I do,' said Mike when the elderly man had left the room.

'That's the Internet for you—as soon as he got the diagnosis he read every leaflet I gave him and then monopolised the library PC to check that I knew what I was talking about.'

Mike stood up. 'Well, you've got my vote. Can I just cast an eye over the surgery's diabetes register?'

Grace waved him towards the PC. 'Help yourself. It's open on one of the windows.'

Evening surgery didn't start until six p.m. on a Thursday. The riding lesson was due to finish at five. After a short struggle with himself, Mike drove to Rivercut Stables despite the fact that Grace had said she'd bring Bethany back. Inside a large, brightly lit barn, a dozen or so little boys and girls were solemnly walking round in a giant circle. There were a sprinkling of parents, a handsome woman in riding breeches lounging to one side of the ring and a couple of others calling instructions. Bethany was perched on a chubby barrel of a pony, being led by Grace.

Mike's heart leapt into his mouth. Bethany looked half entranced, half terrified. When she saw him she let go with one hand and managed a quick wave before grabbing the reins again.

Grace turned, and smiled with delighted approbation. Mike smiled back, his nerves easing. Grace looked good in riding breeches, boots and sweater. In fact, she'd looked good every time he had seen her.

Then he shook himself. Hadn't he decided it would be better if he *didn't* react to Grace as a sexual being? She was a colleague, a friend. It was foolish to mix work and pleasure.

It was nearly the end of the riding lesson. The children were told to give their pony an encouraging pat on the neck. Then they had to dismount, take off the saddle and bridle, and carry them back to the tack room before leading the pony to its stall. The two riding-school ladies trotted up and down the line, keeping an eye on the older ones and showing the newbies what to do. Mike hurried over to carry the saddle, which was far too heavy for Bethany. But his daughter was emphatic that she would lead the pony herself.

Grace kept an unobtrusive hand on the pony's mane as the string ambled out of the barn. 'She did really well,' she said.

'Damn. You mean she wants to carry on?'

'Not a doubt, I'd say. You can buy her the most expensive riding hat in the catalogue if it makes you feel better.'

Mike sighed. 'Sadly, I can't imagine a Christmas present she'd like more.'

The older woman who had been watching from the side broke off her conversation with one of the parents. 'Grace Fellowes. What a surprise. What brings you here?'

Mike saw Grace stiffen. 'I've been leading Bethany Curtis around. She's a new pupil. Dr Curtis, Lorna Threlkeld is the owner of Rivercut Stables.'

Cool eyes assessed him. 'Welcome to Rivercut, Dr Curtis.'

'Thank you, I—'

But the woman behind them had hurried forward. 'Dr Curtis!'

Lorna strolled back into the barn. Mike turned.

The voice belonged to Grace's diabetes patient. 'There, now, I thought I recognised you. Would Bethany like to come to tea tomorrow? I can pick her up from school and you can collect her after surgery.'

Instinctively, Mike looked at Grace. She gave the tiniest nod.

'Thank you, that would be lovely. Bethany, sweetheart, Joanne's mother has invited…'

But he heard Grace's intake of breath and saw her nudge the pony forward. Angela Mather was still talking, holding up the rest of the line, giving him yard-by-yard directions to her house. He nodded and smiled, but his eyes were on Grace. And on the man coming from the car park who had just altered course to cross her path.

The man had the smug air of a chap who was well aware of his own good looks. He was wearing a good suit, good shoes. Mike disliked him on sight. His eyes flicked from Grace to Bethany, to Grace's hand on the pony's mane. 'Supplementing your income playing nursemaid, Grace? Or is it wish fulfilment?' He laughed and went into the barn. A moment later Mike heard him laugh again—and a female laugh tinkle in reply.

Mike strode forward. 'I could thump his teeth down his throat for you, if you like?'

Grace's set face broke into a forced replica of her usual smile. 'Don't bother. He's not worth the grazed knuckles.'

'No, really, I'd like to.'

Her mouth wobbled into a shaky laugh.

He studied her face. 'Are you all right?'

'Me? Never better.'

CHAPTER SIX

GRACE was half expecting the knock on the door.

'Hi,' said Mike in an unconvincing I-was-just-passing tone. 'We didn't realise until bedtime that you still had Bethany's clothes for school.'

As excuses went, it was a pretty good one. 'Sorry,' said Grace, 'I forgot. Here you are.'

But he'd stepped into the cottage's small front room, ignoring the proffered carrier bag, and had shut the door. 'It's all right,' he said, sitting on the sofa. 'I'm not going to loom.'

Grace sighed, accepting the inevitable. 'Coffee? Tea?'

'Whichever will make you feel most comfortable.'

'That'll be tea, then,' she muttered.

'And no sitting on that cushion on the other side of the room either,' he said when she came back in.

Grace put two mugs on the coffee table. 'If

that's your version of "Trust me, I'm a doctor", it needs work.'

Mike smiled. 'You don't need a doctor, you need a friend.' He patted the seat next to him.

Grace sat down. Truth to tell, she had—quite badly—needed an arm around her all evening. 'A friend?' she said.

'A friend. A listening ear. Tell you what, let's start with the woman who owns the stables and carry on from there.'

Grace sipped her tea. 'Lorna Threlkeld? Oh, she's just a minor irritant. Her father is a big landowner around here. He was most put out when Dad sold our farms to the tenants, not to him. He kept ringing up and offering more money, but Dad simply said he was quite well enough off already, thank you, and turned him down every time. So Lorna doesn't like me by way of perpetuating her father's ill-feeling. I can live with it.'

Mike's voice was gentle. 'And the idiot who arrived as we were leaving?'

Her heart gave a sharp twist. 'Yes, well, that was Peter.'

'I hoped it was.'

She looked up at him, startled. 'Hoped? Why?'

He wrapped his arm around her shoulders and gave her a comforting squeeze. 'Because I don't like to think of there being two men who could upset you like that.'

She laughed. 'Thank you. That's very sweet.' She put her mug down on the table and leant against him. It felt comforting and strangely natural. But he was waiting for the story with the air of a man who was prepared to sit there all night if necessary, and this time she was ready to tell him.

'Peter Cox is a local solicitor. He grew up near Nestoby and now he's got a thriving practice based mainly towards Whitby. I've sort of known him for years, but we didn't get together properly until I came back to take up the job here. We went out a few times, bumped into each other at parties, you know how it is.'

'All too well.'

'Anyway, when Mum had her heart attack, he was a real tower of strength, comforting me, saying he'd take care of all the formalities, saying she wouldn't want me to be unhappy. I didn't let him deal with the legal stuff, of course—for one thing we had our own family so-licitor and for another I knew it was a task I must do myself—but I did let him comfort me in other ways. And somehow there we were, engaged, and he said he'd been waiting all his life for a woman like me.' She put up a hand to dash away a tear. 'And I was so happy—in spite of all the awfulness of Mum's death and the mess her affairs were in. I thought… I thought…'

'Shh.' Mike pulled her close and kissed her softly on the forehead. 'What happened next?'

It was a strange way of being kissed. The kiss of a friend. Non-threatening and non-sexual. But she still didn't want to say the next bit. 'Mike, I can't.'

'How about if I help you? That room you didn't want us to see yesterday—it had been decorated a lot more recently than the rest of the house. There was nursery paper with cheerful, smiling animals on the walls. There was fresh paintwork. There were new light fittings, a dimmer switch on the wall, brightly coloured curtains. Grace, it's not difficult to work out.'

Grace felt the tears leaking out of her eyes again. Blast him. Why was he making her dredge this up? 'Yes. Yes, you're right. I was pregnant.

It wasn't planned, but there had been times when we hadn't been very careful during sex, so at the backs of our minds it had always been a possibility. I told Peter and he was thrilled and I was happy about it too. I wanted a family. I longed to bring laughter and love back to the manor. Peter was virtually living with me by then and really enjoyed planning how the manor could be updated, how it could be modernised. It would be luxurious, he said, welcoming and habitable and a lovely home for our children. It was far too early, but we got carried away, We even decided on the name for the first one—Jonathan or Eleanor. And he encouraged me to decorate the nursery. He said I should do it up exactly as I wanted it.'

'Oh, Grace.'

'I worked on the nursery while he drew up plans for the rest of the house and got estimates from builders. The estimates came in, they were expensive but reasonable. I was so happy that he was enjoying the thought of turning the manor into a home again.'

'Then?'

'Then the probate papers arrived. It was what

I'd expected, but I must have made some sort of face when I opened the packet, because Peter asked me what the problem was.'

'He got a shock?'

'A shock! I wondered if I'd have to resuscitate him! His mouth opened and shut for a minute, but no sound came out. My family had been almost rich before my mother's second husband came along. Not any more. Poor Peter was horrified. He'd thought he was marrying money. And it transpired that when he'd said he'd see to all the renovations himself, he hadn't meant that he'd pay for them, he'd meant he'd supervise them. He yelled and shouted and said I'd led him on—letting him think I had money when all the time I wanted his.'

Mike's grip around her shoulders tightened. 'Bastard.'

'I said I couldn't believe he hadn't already known. The rest of the village had got wind of it. Why did he think Mum had had her seizure, for goodness' sake? And I knew I'd wept all over his silk shirts about the whole thing. He said I'd taken care to be incomprehensible while I was sobbing. What he meant was that he hadn't been listening.'

'A man who hears what he wants to hear, in other words.'

'You've got it.' Grace fumbled for a tissue and blew her nose. 'He stormed back to his own place, and for the first time ever I had to phone your father and tell him I couldn't work that day. I felt dreadful. I was shivering, nauseous, I couldn't stop crying, I had a blinding headache and appalling stomach cramps. I fell asleep out of sheer nervous exhaustion. And when I woke up, I realised I was having a miscarriage.'

'Oh, Grace.' He hugged her tight. 'You poor thing. You must have been devastated.'

'I was. And to make things worse, he went around telling people that I'd tried to trap him. That I wanted his money and had got pregnant to force him into marriage. But lucky for him…'

Mike swore, long and comprehensively. Listening to him, Grace felt surprisingly better.

'It's all right. Really. I won't say it hasn't left a scar, but I'm fine now. I'm just very glad I found out what Peter was like before I married him. In that way I was luckier than my mother.'

'Grace, only you could find a bright side in that experience.'

'Well, I don't think I'll ever be quite so trusting again. But none of the folk in Rivercut believed him. The good things in life still outweigh the bad.'

'Humph,' said Mike. 'What was he doing at the stables? Are we going to meet him every time Bethany goes riding?'

'I doubt it. He's Lorna's father's solicitor. I expect he was there on a matter of business. Lorna isn't usually there herself. She lets her staff see to the running of the place.'

'Those two instructors we saw? They seemed nice.'

'They are.' Then his words filtered through. 'What do you mean, "Are *we* going to meet him?" I'm supposed to be paying off my tyres, taking Bethany riding. I thought you couldn't bear to watch?'

'I can't. Not for the whole time. I was being brave this afternoon.'

She smiled up at him. 'You did very well. I was proud of you.'

He looked down at her. 'You were?' he said, an odd note in his voice.

Their faces were very close. Grace felt a small tremor run through her. 'I was,' she said.

The next bit happened in slow motion. Very tentatively, Mike bent his head. Grace found herself stretching up to meet him. As she felt his lips on hers, felt the warmth of his body, the strength of his arms as they tightened around her, she knew that this was more than Mike trying to comfort her. It was the kiss of a lover for a lover, a kiss promising everything. She could stop him if she wanted to, but she didn't want to stop him at all.

He pulled her closer. She eased herself towards him and slid her arm around his waist. His hand cupped the back of her head as his kiss became deeper, more intense. She found herself exploring his mouth as eagerly as he was exploring hers, and she gave an inarticulate murmur at the unexpected excitement it generated in her. Her body moved against his; it was telling her that this was good, this was wonderful, that she needed more and…

She pulled back, breathing fast. What was she *doing*?

He understood the message at once. He slackened his hold. 'That… That was…so good,' he said, just as the silence got beyond bearable.

'Mike, I…' She broke off. 'Oh, Mike. I don't know.'

'Grace…'

She shook her head. 'Don't say anything.'

'I have to. Grace, I didn't intend that. I don't know why I did it.' He hesitated. 'But I'd like to do it again.'

Without another word they came together for a second kiss. This was less tentative. Their mouths had already accepted each other. Grace felt herself tingle all over as her tongue twined with his, as she learnt the shape of his lips—both strange and immediately familiar. It was just a kiss, just holding each other and kissing. It ended naturally, with a lingering reluctance. There could have been so much more—part of her wanted so much more—but it was too soon.

Grace knew she would have to explain something of what she felt. But how to find the words when she didn't understand herself? She put a hand to his cheek, meeting his eyes squarely and openly. 'Mike, that was lovely—more than lovely—but I don't think I'm ready for it and I'm fairly sure you aren't either. Can we leave it like this for now? Can we be just friends?'

He took a ragged breath. 'I'm not sure we can. Not after that. Not after the way you made me feel then. But we can try.'

For a moment more she leant against him, secure in his hold, the memory of the kiss still with her. 'We've only just met,' she said, as much to herself as to him. 'We barely know each other. I'm scarred. You're still wounded. You are, aren't you?'

He passed a hand across his eyes. 'Grace, I can't not be honest with you,' he said slowly. 'Yes I miss Sarah. How can I not? I loved her very much. But while I was kissing you there was no one in my head but you and nowhere else in the world that I wanted to be but right here on your sofa. So I'm feeling guilty now because I didn't feel guilty then. And that's not fair on you.'

She nodded, still tucked into his side. 'Look at us,' she said softly, 'we're like two birds with broken wings. We can flap and make a lot of noise—but we can't fly.'

'Broken wings do mend,' he told her. 'Perhaps we'll learn to fly again.'

'I hope so. I really do.'

* * *

Mike strode out into the night, hoping the cold air would cool his brain. What had he been thinking of? How could he have lost his wits so thoroughly? A snowflake melted on his eyelid, several snowflakes. He groaned. He'd come out without a hat—a fine one he'd been this morning to lecture Bethany about wrapping up warmly. *Bethany. Sarah. Grace.* Oh, Lord, what a tangle.

He heard footsteps thudding in the snow behind him, and a voice calling his name. 'Mike—you forgot this.'

He turned to see Grace in flapping duffle coat with a woolly hat jammed on her head, holding out the bag containing Bethany's clothes. He gave a shamed laugh. 'I must have had something on my mind.'

'Don't let it give you sleepless nights,' she said with a smile.

The falling snow made the village look like a scene from a Christmas card. Lights blazing out of the narrow windows of St Lawrence's church simply added to the illusion. As they stood there the choir began to rehearse another carol, 'Good King Wenceslas'.

'They must have timed that on purpose,' Grace

said. 'Listen, "When the snow lay round about. Deep and crisp and even."'

Mike laughed. 'It's not like this in London, you know. In fact, much more of this weather and it'll be "In the Deep Midwinter". How d'you fancy driving when there's water like a stone?'

She grinned. 'I've got new tyres. I can drive anywhere.' Then reached up and kissed his cheek, before turning and hurrying back to her cottage.

Despite her admonition, he did wake up in the small hours thinking of her. He'd been dreaming of Sarah, dreaming of holding her asleep—she'd used to sleep in such a fierce, concentrated way—but when he woke it was Grace in his head and Grace's lips in his memory. He lay there, aching and not knowing why, for a long time before his eyes closed again and he drifted off.

He only saw Grace briefly on Friday. She'd popped in between visits to supplement her medical kit before heading back out again.

'Grace,' he said, hurrying outside after her. 'I was wondering what you were doing at the weekend. Bethany and I are going house hunting. The estate agent has sent us a list, but a couple of the locations look pretty inaccessible without local knowledge.'

She smiled at him as she stowed her kit in the back of the Land Rover. 'Sorry, I can't help. I'm off to a nursing reunion in Leeds. You'd better take your father with you instead.'

His face must have registered his surprise. She grinned. 'Don't look so injured. I do have a life, Mike.'

'I suppose you must have. Oh, well, enjoy yourself.'

'I'll do my best.'

He glanced at the rear of the car. 'Good grief, you're not camping, are you?'

'No, I'm staying with my old roommate. She married a local doctor and still lives in Leeds.' She followed his gaze and laughed. 'That's my out-in-the-snow survival kit. Sleeping bag, reflective blanket. Thermos. Chocolate, Kendal mint cake, thick socks... You ought to have something similar—especially driving Bethany around. Ask James what you need.'

It was a good thought. 'I will. Thanks for the tip. Wait a moment. You'd better give me your mobile number—just in case.'

She raised her eyebrows. 'In case of what? If my patients have an emergency, they need you, your father or the ambulance, not me.' But she gave it to him anyway, and then at his insistence added his mobile number to her phone's address book. 'See you Monday, Mike.'

They had now seen four properties and none of them had been right. Driving back through the falling dusk on Saturday afternoon, Mike reflected gloomily that at this rate Bethany would have grown up and left home before they'd moved out of his father's surgery flat.

'I know it needed work, but it was a good size for its price, that last one,' said James.

Mike wasn't convinced. He drew to a stop outside the estate agent's office to drop the keys off. 'You two stay in the car. No point all of us getting cold.'

'Sorry,' he said to the agent's polite enquiry. 'Too far out, too cramped, too lonely and too dilapidated in that order.'

The agent accepted this philosophically. 'You're sure you can't go higher on price?' he asked. 'I do have something—perhaps bigger than you were envisaging—but it's slightly over your maximum.' He turned to rummage in a filing cabinet. 'It's a very superior property actually in Rivercut, which, if I remember, was one of your main requirements. It would benefit from a little modernisation, but I assure you it is perfectly habitable.' He found the details and drew them out, tapping the pages in an unde-cided manner. 'I don't know... My colleague has had one or two nibbles—a local landowner is most interested—but if you are in the position to make a cash purchase... The owner is desirous of selling as soon as possible.'

Mike shrugged and held out his hand. 'I may as well take a look. I can always say no, can't I?'

'Indeed, yes, sir. Good evening.'

Mike took the brochure and hurried back to the car. He wanted to get back home, he wanted warm food inside Bethany and a hot mug of coffee inside himself. He dropped the house details on his father's lap and started the car. And then stalled with a jerk as he caught sight of the photo of the property. 'That's the manor,' he said, flabbergasted.

James looked down. 'I did tell you Grace was having to sell.'

Yes, he had, and Mike knew it perfectly well,

really. It was simply that he thought of the manor as Grace's house. She had fitted the place so well—worn it like a ballgown, to use her own analogy. The stark reality of her situation honestly hadn't struck him until he saw that colour photograph, flat and businesslike on the top sheet of the agent's property details.

It was Grace's house. Anyone buying it would be an interloper. Yes, she'd be solvent again, but how would she feel, seeing someone else parked in the driveway? How would she feel, seeing builders' trucks outside? Hearing the crash and rumble of internal walls being demolished and rebuilt into quite a different floor plan? Catching glimpses of skips on jolting lorries, brimming over with old, cracked Victorian bathroom fittings?

It wasn't to be borne.

And she didn't need to bear it.

If James noticed that his son was quiet for the rest of the evening, he didn't mention it. In truth, Mike had already made his decision. Buying the manor may not have occurred to him before, but as soon as it had all that remained was for him to work out how.

* * *

Grace arrived home just after lunch on Sunday. Or, rather, just after when her friend Natalie's lunch would have been. She'd been pressed to stay, but she'd said she wanted to get back in daylight. Nobody queried the fact that a good proportion of her working life was spent negotiating lonely moorland roads with the aid of her headlights. It had been a good weekend. She'd enjoyed staying with Natalie and spending time with Chloe, her god-daughter. She'd had fun meeting up with the old crowd, catching up with what they were all doing. But she'd stopped drinking as soon as she'd started seeing Mike's face everywhere, and now she was home with presents to put under her tree, looking forward to a bowl of home-made soup and a satisfying session of Christmas decorating. It did give her a nasty moment, driving past the manor and seeing car tracks and footprints in the snow, but she told herself she was being ridiculous. Just think how much better off she'd be without the mortgage payments emptying her account every month. She pulled up outside the cottage and took a deep breath. Right, first the soup, then she would get the tree in.

* * *

Mike walked down the drive of the manor, mulling things over in his mind. It was bigger than the sort of place he'd envisioned buying, but it had land for Bethany to run in and she would love it. He stopped and turned back to gaze at the facade. It was a jewel—perfectly in proportion—he'd be a fool not to buy it. But, and it was a big but, what about Grace?

He resumed his progress through the snow. It was getting cold again and the parts that had turned to slush were freezing. He hoped Grace would take care driving back from Leeds. And on that thought, he saw her Land Rover parked snugly outside her cottage! Mike was amazed at the rush of gladness that filled him. Pleasure that she was back in Rivercut where she belonged. Thankful that she'd made it across the country without mishap.

Then he got the shock of his life. The tall, bushy tree by the corner of her house moved across to the front door by itself! What the…?

'Come on,' said the tree, pushing into the aperture. 'Let's see if you fit *this* way.'

Mike let out a shout of laughter and hurried around the car to give Grace a hand. 'Do you know your Christmas tree sounds just like you?' he said.

Grace was wearing her duffle coat and had gloves on. Both arms were wrapped around the trunk. 'It should,' she said with a grunt. 'I've had it fifteen years now. Come on, tree, don't get stuck *there*.'

Mike hastily propped up the very hefty mid-section and got a shoulder full of pine needles as a thank you. 'Perhaps you could ask it to breathe in,' he suggested. 'Or buy it a diet book. Grace, this is too big for the doorway.'

'It isn't. It's just a case of getting the angle right.'

From what Mike could see she was braced on the other side of the door, pulling for all she was worth. He sighed and felt through the branches, trying to get a purchase. 'Ouch, this tree's dangerous!'

'That's why I've got gloves on.'

'Grace—have you thought that even if we get it into the room, you're not going to have anywhere to stand it?'

'I've moved the big cushion.' She heaved again and he heard a shower of earth tip out of the pot.

Mike stopped trying to feed the branches one

by one through the doorway. 'This is silly. You're trying to fit a manor-sized tree into a cottage. You think *I* loom when I'm standing in your front room? This will fill it! You'll have to clamber across the furniture to get from the stairs to the kitchen.' He shifted his grip and a branch took the opportunity to slap him across the face. 'And the scent will be overpowering.'

'I like pine,' said Grace, sounding muffled.

'There's a difference between liking pine and living in a tree house!'

Silence. Then a sniff. Mike cursed, let go of the tree and pelted around the side of the cottage to the back door. He threaded his way through a tiny kitchen and found Grace with a green streak on her forehead, pine needles in her hair and a tear rolling down her cheek.

'Oh, Grace,' he said, and wrapped his arms around her, just as he might with Bethany when she'd been trying so hard to tie her own shoe-laces and hadn't managed it.

'My father gave me this tree,' she said, a quiver in her voice. 'To replace the one he gave me when I was little for my very own because I loved Christmas so much. That one died. But this one's good and strong and I brought it with me so I'd have something of him. I've lost so much, Mike…'

He held her tighter. 'Shh. I've got an idea. Why don't we stand this tree outside your front door, so you can put lights on it the way the manor trees were always decorated in that photo you showed me? Then the villagers will know you're keeping the tradition alive. And we can go over to the place you told me about and buy you a *small* tree for inside the cottage.'

In the circle of his arms, he felt her let out a half-sigh. 'I suppose you think I should have thought of that for myself.'

He hugged her quickly and released her. 'We aren't always very sensible when grief is involved. How far is the Christmas tree place? I'll come with you now if you like. Then I'll know the way for when I take Bethany to choose one.'

'You don't have to.'

'Oh, I think I do. You obviously have zero spatial awareness. I need to stand next to all the trees on offer so you can find one that won't loom at you.'

She turned out to be a good driver, considerate and careful even when she wasn't being followed in a Range Rover. It might not be the most comfortable of vehicles, but Mike felt himself relax, knowing she was safe to be out on the hills in all weathers. He was glad he hadn't given in to the urge to kiss her again. Or at least only one soft kiss on her hair that he didn't think she'd noticed. It was much better to keep things friendly between them.

On the way back she glanced towards the manor. Mike guessed she did it habitually. 'I'll have to go and collect the outside lights,' she murmured, 'and maybe other bits as well. The estate agent left a message on my mobile yesterday to say someone had made an offer. It's a lot lower than I was asking, but it might be worth it, just to get rid of the mortgage.'

Yesterday? That had been before he'd viewed it officially, before he'd even been given the details! 'No,' he said before he could stop himself. 'Don't accept. It's a bargain just as it is.'

She turned a laughing face to him. 'Mike, it isn't. The central heating costs an absolute fortune to run, the plumbing needs modernising, the electrics badly need rewiring and the kitchen is well overdue for the biggest makeover in the world. And the whole place should be redecorated.'

'But the roof is sound, it didn't feel damp the other day, and it has mistletoe in the garden. The manor is a gem, Grace. When the right person comes along and falls in love with it, they'll pay the asking price.'

'Will that be before or after I go bankrupt?'

'Before,' Mike said firmly. 'Let's fetch your string of lights now before it gets dark and we electrocute ourselves on the dodgy wiring.'

As they entered the manor, Mike watched Grace's face. He felt her love for the place. Her smile was half sad, half happy memory.

'Oh, Grace,' he said. 'How are you going to feel with someone else living here? This was a good home for you.'

She walked resolutely up the stairs. When she spoke her voice was stronger. 'I loved it here. I hope whoever buys it will love it just as much.'

It was no good, he was going to have to say something soon. If only he knew how she would really feel!

CHAPTER SEVEN

AFTER the third patient in a row told Mike on Monday morning that they'd no doubt see him at the party, he thought it might be an idea to ring Grace.

'Which party?' he said, trying not to let a plaintive tone into his voice.

She chuckled down the phone. He could hear her walking briskly along. 'The children's one. In the village hall tomorrow afternoon after school. Angela Mather told you about it, remember?'

'Angela Mather. Type 1 diabetic. Joanne's mother. Talks.'

'That's her. Also party organiser.'

Mike remembered something else. 'Sausage rolls!' he said, aghast. 'Do they sell them at the village shop?'

'Mike, you can't send Bethany to her first

Rivercut party with shop-bought sausage rolls! It's a matter of honour.'

'The children won't notice,' Mike protested.

'The mothers will. And you're an honorary mother.'

Mike leaned his head against the window pane. 'Dear Grace, if you are not doing anything when you finish work, you wouldn't like to come and construct sausage rolls with Bethany in our kitchen, would you? I can offer you supper. Dad makes a mean casserole.'

'How can I resist? I'll buy the ingredients while I'm doing my rounds, shall I?'

Mike sighed. 'Yes, please.'

Grace arrived that evening, put down a promisingly bulging bag and started divesting herself of her outer garments. 'Oh, it's lovely to be warm,' she said, getting her hair caught as she unwound her scarf. 'One of the reasons I enjoy farm visits so much is that I mostly see patients in the farmhouse kitchen, with the Aga permanently on and wonderful smells seeping out of the oven. It's a shame modern houses don't have kitchens big enough to really live in.' She was wearing a big floppy sweater under her coat, but stripped it off in a double-overarm movement to reveal a figure-hugging dark blue angora jumper underneath. It had a V-neck and three-quarter sleeves and made Mike wonder very much what the layer below that was like.

He blinked as Grace produced a spray cleaner from her bag, squirted the table and wiped it with a kitchen towel. Then she gave the spray to Bethany, telling her to do her side as well, all the time explaining bacteria in terms a five-year-old could understand.

Mike was impressed. He poured out three glasses of Rioja, took one through to his father, who was shouting points of medical procedure at a TV hospital soap. When he came back Bethany was wrapped in a cook's apron, had just had her hands washed and was installed at the table to weigh out the flour and margarine. Mike leaned against the worktop, ready to be amused.

Grace narrowed her eyes. 'Now, then, is this fair?' she asked Bethany. 'Us doing all the work and Daddy just standing there, drinking a glass of wine?'

'You've got a glass of wine too,' he pointed out.

'Daddy, help,' decreed Bethany.

'I haven't got an apron,' he said cunningly.

Grace crossed to her bag, pulled out a blue-and-white-striped barbeque number and dropped the neck loop over his head. For a moment she was standing very close to him. 'You planned that,' he said, an unexpected tightness in his chest.

She grinned. 'Would I do such a thing? Okay, here we are. Sausage rolls.'

She had a children's recipe book with her, with big clear writing and step-by-step photos. 'You didn't buy it especially, did you?' said Mike, worried about her spending money she didn't have.

'No, I picked it up at the last church sale. I was going to give it to my god-daughter, but when I got there last weekend, I saw it on Natalie's kitchen shelf already. I'll leave it here for Bethany if you like.'

This was fun. Bethany's first two attempts at scooping flour out of the bag into the measuring bowl resulted in a small-scale snowdrift on the table.

'It'll be useful for rolling out the pastry,' said Grace, unperturbed. 'Shall we let Daddy have the next turn?' She reached for the scoop at the same time as Mike. She drew back at once, but he thought she'd probably felt the same frisson that had run through him during the brief moment when the backs of their hands touched.

By the time there was enough in the mixing bowl there was flour everywhere, but Bethany had learnt what the gradations on the scale meant in real terms—in a way Mike doubted she'd have managed at school. Grace was really good with children. And when he caught himself drawing a fancy pattern on the pastry with a zigzag roller, he suspected she might be good with him too. All the same, the sausage rolls were a lumpy, misshapen lot. 'Shall I buy some from the shop anyway?' he asked in a low tone as she put the tray in the oven.

'Certainly not. These have got character. Besides, kids aren't bothered what things look like at a party, just what they taste like.'

'If you say so. Oh, Lord, look at this place. Bethany, sweetheart, I think I'd better put you in the bath clothes and all tonight.'

His daughter giggled. The apron had kept most of her clean, but she had flour in her hair, flour and margarine and sausage meat on her hands and suspicious bits of pastry around her mouth.

'You can talk,' said Grace, carrying Bethany to the sink and rinsing her hands.

'What do you mean?'

'Well, let's just say you're going to look very distinguished when you're older.'

Mike hastened to the mirror in the hall. He appeared to have gone grey at the temples since they'd started baking. 'Could be worse. Go and sit with Grandad while we clean up, darling.'

Grace scrubbed efficiently at the table. Mike fetched a broom for the floor. 'Wait a minute,' he said. 'Take off your apron.'

Grace looked at him in surprise, but undid the ties. A small shower of flour fell from behind the bib to the floor. She tutted and brushed at her jumper. The white streaks became more pronounced.

'No, don't. You've got damp hands. You're making it worse. Here, let me.'

He brushed the loose flour away from her midriff. Her angora jumper was soft to the touch, and warm where it lay against her body. Grace, however, had gone suddenly still. 'Lift your arm,' he said, and very, very carefully he brushed the flour away from her side, his fingers tantalisingly close to the swell of her breast. 'There's, um, more…'

'Go on, then,' she invited softly. Her breath was coming slightly faster and the pupils of her eyes had dilated. Then the oven timer broke into a flurry of beeping, sending them instantly to either side of the kitchen.

'There,' said Grace, clattering the tray down with a hand that wasn't quite so steady as normal. 'A beautiful batch of sausage rolls.'

Surprisingly, they did smell wonderful. As Bethany and James both bounded in to sample them, Mike hoped his father would put his heightened colour down to the heat from the stove.

It had been a lovely evening, thought Grace. The moments alone with Mike in the kitchen had been especially lovely. After the baking she'd helped bathe Bethany and agreed with her choice of a pretty pink full-skirted dress for tomorrow's party. She'd also been shown her 'Adventure Calendar'—'Every day I can open a window and there's a chocolate inside, but I mustn't open two windows at once and get two chocolates'—and read a bedtime story.

After that Grace had eaten James's casserole and drunk another glass of Mike's Rioja and now Mike was walking her home.

'There's no need,' she'd said, but he claimed he wanted a stroll to clear his head so he may as well stroll in the direction of her cottage. Grace wondered what was coming next. She wasn't at all sure that she wanted things to move too fast.

They walked side by side, not touching, talking of nothing in particular. Mike had his hands in his pockets. He seemed to have something on his mind that hadn't been there earlier in the evening. They reached her cottage and stopped. She hadn't quite decided whether to invite him in for a coffee when he spoke abruptly.

'I've got to ask you something, Grace. If I leave it any longer, it's going to get too difficult and I won't know how to say it at all.'

Grace was apprehensive now. What did he mean?

'You know Bethany and I were house hunting over the weekend?'

'Yes. Did you find anything?'

'Sort of. It hadn't occurred to me at first. But

there's nothing else, and the more I thought about it, the more I realised it would be perfect.'

'Mike, what are you talking about?'

He slapped his forehead. 'I am making such a mess of this. Grace, how would you feel about me buying the manor?'

Grace's mouth fell open. It was the last thing she'd expected him to say.

He groaned. 'You hate the idea. I don't blame you. It's *your* house—it would be like evicting you.'

She found her voice. 'No,' she said slowly. 'No, I don't hate the idea. I mean, it is for sale. I need the cash, it's owed to other people. Someone's got to buy it. And I evicted myself because I couldn't afford to run it. That central heating just *eats* money.'

'Yes, but we have to work together. You'll see me several times a week at close quarters, not just passing in the road. I think what I'm saying is would you mind if I was the new owner? Would you be upset when you saw me driving out of what used to be your drive? Or if I invited you for a cup of tea in what used to be your living room?'

'It would be odd, certainly. But it would be odd with anybody.' He looked so distressed that she put her hand on his arm to reassure him, still not sure of what she really felt herself. 'I think you would at least be sympathetic to the renovations it needs. But, Mike, they'll cost a fortune.'

He smiled briefly. 'I've got sufficient funds, Grace.'

'If you're serious… Oh, Mike, I don't know. I think I'd rather it went to a friend than a complete stranger. And I'd love to think of Bethany growing up there.'

'Then shall I do it? Contact the estate agent in the morning?'

'Yes. If you're sure.' And because she didn't know how to say the next bit, she let her hand slip down to squeeze his wrist. 'Mike, I won't invite you in. Not because of you buying the manor. Not because of anything that might have happened earlier, which felt…nice. Just because it's been a really lovely evening and I don't want it to get…messy.'

He smiled. 'It *has* been a nice evening, hasn't it? Thank you.' He hesitated, then kissed her cheek and left, striding back up the high street.

Grace went indoors, her thoughts all over the place. Mike at the manor. It was an awfully large house just for him and Bethany. But she recalled he'd been in with a big crowd in London—his partners and their families, his wife's friends. They'd all pitched in when Sarah had died. Kept him going, looked after Bethany. No doubt they would be coming up to stay from time to time. Sleeping in the guest bedrooms, cooking in the kitchen, having drinks in the hall, their children playing in the gardens with Bethany.

It would be strange to have the manor full again and her not there. And she wondered if any of those friends were single, just waiting for Mike to stop grieving.

This was no good! What should have been uppermost in her mind was that soon she would be free of debt, free of responsibility. She could start to plan her life again. But mostly what she was thinking about was Mike's kiss on her cheek—and the thrilling touch of his hand on her body.

The waiting room was full when Mike arrived from taking Bethany to school. James always started his appointments at eight-thirty, but Mike had been amazed at how no one—surgery staff and patients alike—expected Mike himself to begin until after he'd got back from Rivercut Primary. Even so, he rang through to Grace's room before telling the receptionist he was ready.

'I know you're in the middle of a clinic, but I just wanted to know whether it was still all right for me to go ahead with the manor?'

'It's still all right.'

'Good. Don't run away at lunchtime. Have a sandwich with Dad and me. I need to know what else I'm supposed to do for the party.'

'Very well, Dr Curtis.'

Mike smiled as he buzzed for his first patient. He loved Grace's 'official' voice.

He was surprised later when she put a small present, wrapped in Christmas paper, on the kitchen table. 'Is that for thanking me for buying the manor? There ought to be a message for you from the estate agent, by the way.'

'There has been and I said yes. *This* is to go under the Christmas tree at the party. Each child puts one there and they take a different one home with them.'

'That's a nice idea. You must tell me how much I owe you.'

She grinned and pointed to the receipts tucked discreetly under the parcel.

James bustled in. 'Tut, tut, no one got the kettle on yet? I'm parched. I've had Mrs Carter in talking at me. Says she's worried about Nina. Seems she's started getting secretive and hiding things from her and sometimes she giggles for no reason at all and did I think she could be taking drugs?'

Grace laughed. 'Oh, dear, what did you say?'

'I said she was a healthy nineteen-year-old with a good job and a refreshingly honest take on life and I didn't think Mrs Carter needed to worry. I *didn't* say that if Mrs Carter herself had taken what I very much hope young Nina is on, there would be rather fewer Carter offspring mopping up the buffet at the Rivercut children's party this afternoon.'

It was nice, having Grace there. His dad was obviously fond of her and as she talked over a couple of cases with them, Mike could again see just how good a nurse she was. He wondered if he could make the sharing of lunchtime sandwiches a routine on her surgery days. Then he got a callout, and she looked at her watch in horror and bolted the last of her tea, saying she was late for Mr Blenkinsop's blood-pressure check and Mike remembered all over again why medical personnel bought more indigestion tablets than any other profession in the country.

'See you at the party,' she said as she hurried out. 'Don't be late.'

Far from being late, Bethany was so eager to be gone that they were early at the village hall. She was buzzing with excitement. There were fairy lights, a large Christmas tree and a decorated chair all ready for Father Christmas. There were even Christmas songs belting out of the loudspeakers.

A handful of mothers were busy putting the final touches to the decorations. Mike was surprised to see Grace amongst them, a mound of paper chains in her arms.

'Mike,' she said cheerfully, 'just the man we want.'

'You need a doctor?'

'No, we need someone tall. Could you get the stepladder from under the stage and loop these paper chains round the back of the light fittings and down each side of the hall, please? Then hang the big pictures of Father Christmas underneath the lights.'

'Can do,' said Mike. 'Can someone watch—?' But Bethany was confidently running over to join a couple of little girls from school. No problem there. Other assorted parents were going backwards and forwards, laying out food on the white-covered trestle tables, arranging jugs of squash and plastic cups, counting rows of tiny presents and frowning over lists. The mothers smiled at him briefly. The fathers rolled their eyes. This was obviously not a time for standing around chatting.

Mike got on with his paper chains. 'Brilliant,' said Grace, appearing by his side. 'Tea's up, everyone. Grab a cup while it's hot, the kids will all be arriving in a few minutes. And give yourselves a pat on the back too. The place looks wonderful.'

'Let's hope the little darlings appreciate it,' said a passing mother. She gave Mike a friendly smile. 'Come on, the tea urn is this way.'

Mike glanced around for Bethany. Grace had

moved over to the children and was keeping an eye on them.

'Dr Curtis, isn't it?' continued the mother, leading him towards the kitchen behind the stage. 'I understand there is no Mrs Curtis?'

'No,' said Mike, 'not now.' He marvelled at the efficiency of village gossip.

'Ah, well, we're a friendly bunch here. Let me introduce you to a few people…'

He found that he was expected—and that he wanted—to stay. He watched one or two party games and saw that Bethany, as always, was enjoying herself. It struck him that the Rivercut mothers were in essence no different from the ones in his London crowd. They pulled together, looked after solitary males in their midst with kind efficiency, organised themselves to cover all bases. No one person was doing all the work.

'This village is better organised than the Mafia,' he said to Grace, finding himself standing next to her later.

'Except there's no vow of silence,' she said with a laugh.

She had taken off the apron that had covered her dress—and her dress was wonderful. Simple, in a blue silky material, it did nothing but show off her figure. And that figure was gorgeous. 'How do you come to be involved in all this?' he asked, trying to disguise the fact that he was appreciating her body rather more than was seemly.

'We always used to hold the children's Christmas party up at the manor. The last couple of years... Well, let's just say it's been more sensible to move it down here. But everybody has always taken turns to do the games and swap around doling out food and drink. It's my game next, and then tea.' She cocked her head at him. 'Are you enjoying yourself?'

'Very much. It's nice being a dad today, not a doctor. Everybody is making me feel welcome. What game are you doing?'

She laughed. 'An incredibly ancient Pin the Tail on the Donkey. We have to have it before tea, otherwise the kids throw up when we spin them round. Would you like to help me?'

'I'd love to,' he said. And meant it.

But suddenly there was a shout that was a little louder than the general noise in the hall. People began moving to the far end of the room and a woman's voice was raised in a terrified wail.

'Help him, someone, help him!' There were other confused shouts and even as Mike started running, Grace alongside him, he heard the words, 'Turn him upside down… No, thump him on the back…'

'Let me through,' shouted Mike, adding the time-honoured words, 'I'm a doctor.'

A hysterical woman was clutching a boy aged about four. She looked up at Mike and sobbed, 'It was that cake, the big one with the silver balls on top. I told him he wasn't to touch, but he got one and when I saw he had it he put it in his mouth and now he can't breathe and I've tried banging his back and…'

'Give him to me. What's his name?'

'Alex.'

Mike took Alex, turned him for a quick look at his face. It was turning blue, cyanosis already obvious so the blockage must be nearly complete. Alex was pawing weakly at his throat.

'Did anyone try smacking his back?'

'I did,' a woman volunteered, 'about ten times. But not too hard.'

'Good.' The first step when trying to deal with asphyxiation caused by a foreign body in the trachea was a set of blows to the back. An old remedy, sometimes it worked—but not this time.

Alex was only small, light-boned. Mike turned him around, wrapped his arms round the tiny waist, positioned his hands on the bottom of the diaphragm. The Heimlich manoeuvre. Jerk the hands into the abdomen so the blockage is forced out. But with the weak bones and muscles of a four-year-old child, it was essential not to pull too hard.

Mike ran his fingers up and down the ribcage, felt the softness of the abdomen, tried to assess just how hard he should pull. Now! No result, not hard enough.

He had to remain calm, to think the almost unthinkable. If this didn't work then he might have to perform an emergency tracheotomy. Use whatever knife was handy, cut a hole through the throat into the thorax and use some kind of tube—even a ball point barrel would do—to make an airway. But, please, not yet!

Try again, a little harder. Now! And this time it was exactly right. A silver ball shot onto the floor, the first great shuddering breath was taken, the blue tinge started to fade at once.

There was a huge sigh of relief from the collected parents. The hall, which had been eerily silent, burst into life again.

'Result,' said Mike, feeling the adrenalin in his body die down. 'Now take him somewhere quiet, give him a drink and let him rest for a few minutes. I'll come and have another look at him.'

He turned to the circle of his audience. 'Everything's fine, folks. Alex will be as good as new in five minutes. Let's get on with the party.'

Alex was led away by his grateful mother, but there was another white-faced woman in the crowd. 'It was safe,' she said, her voice getting higher. 'The bag said they were safe to eat.' She was clutching Grace's arm, shaking. 'What if he'd died…?'

'Of course they're safe,' Grace reassured her. 'Pauline, you've been making beautiful village cakes for years and no one's ever had an accident before. Maybe the silver ball Alex grabbed was a bit bigger than the rest. Maybe it got stuck to a lump of icing. As long as we tell the children to crunch and chew properly when it comes to teatime, there won't be a problem. Now, I'm going to do Pin the Tail any minute, so can you put the urn on for the parents' cuppas? Then it will all be ready and people won't have to wait.'

As he crossed the room to help hang up the donkey and get the Victorian tails out of their tissue paper, Mike was struck dumb by Grace's humaneness. Yes, he had saved Alex's life—but Grace had known who'd made the cake. She'd known how the woman would feel and had been there on the spot to administer sensible comfort and a distraction technique.

The party continued, but with a difference. During tea and the last few games, most of the parents found a moment to come up to Mike and say what a good job he'd done.

'You aren't an incomer any more,' said Grace as they got the children settled down and dimmed the lights to wait for Santa. 'You're accepted.'

Every child got a present from Father Christmas, chose another one from under the Christmas tree and started putting coats on to go home. Bethany wanted a goodbye cuddle from Grace.

'Off you go, poppet,' said Grace. 'I'll see you on Thursday for riding.' And to Mike, 'Thanks for your help, even if it was a baptism of fire.'

'I enjoyed it—well, apart from the emergency.

Come back with us, if you like. There's still some of that Rioja left.'

'No, I'll just finish tidying up here, then go home. I'm a bit shattered.'

It was snowing again. Mike lifted Bethany up onto his shoulders for the walk back. She'd had a wonderful time. She had got a fairy wand from Santa—all pink ribbons and glitter—and insisted on waving it around her head, putting magic spells on all the houses they passed. As soon as they got back she had to tell Grandad all about the party.

James chuckled, but looked at Mike shrewdly. 'What's up?'

'I had to perform a Heimlich manoeuvre on a little boy.' He passed a hand over his face. Suddenly he too was shattered. 'Look, Dad, are you all right to do Bethany's bedtime? I left Grace tidying up and I just want to have a word with her.'

'She works too hard, that girl. Why don't you take her to the Coach and Horses for a meal? It does lovely food.'

'Good idea. Thanks, Dad.'

He found Grace alone when he got back to the village hall. She had moved the trestle tables, was sweeping where they had been. He didn't say anything, but found a black bag and started to collect the abandoned plastic plates, cutlery and cups that had been left around.

'There's no need,' said Grace. 'A couple of the others are coming back to help.'

'I need to wind down,' said Mike. 'Bethany's reliving the whole party for Dad.'

'That was a great job you did on Alex. You were so *fast*.'

'Thank God it worked. And you did a good job with the cake-maker too.'

'Poor Pauline. She was horrified.'

'You are one special nurse, you know that? Grace, things are happening fast and I need some time out. Will you come to the pub with me when we've finished this? Dad says the food is good there.'

For a moment he thought she was going to refuse. Then she smiled tiredly at him. 'Time out? That sounds very restful. Thank you. I'd love to.'

CHAPTER EIGHT

GRACE felt her tension drain away as soon as they walked through the door of the Coach and Horses. The pub was warm, full, bright with decorations and a welcoming fire and cosy with good cheer. The Christmas spirit was alive and well. As they threaded their way to a corner table, they got nods and greetings. 'Evening, Grace. Evening, Doctor.'

Mike grinned. 'I've a feeling I should have come in before. Now, then, first a drink, then a bit of business. Then we can relax. What would you like?'

'A red wine, please.' She watched him cross the room and discuss options with the bartender, scanning the shelves with a considering look. He came back with a bottle, two glasses and the menu.

'Cheers,' he said, pouring them each a ruby-red glassful.

It tasted wonderful, soft and rich. 'Cheers,' she replied. 'So, what's this matter of business?'

'The manor,' he said. 'It's going to take the solicitors a while to get their act together and produce contracts for us to sign. I've no idea why it should, but it always does. But I really want to make a start on things now. Overhauling the central heating, for instance. Refitting the kitchen. Getting quotes on a conservatory. What I'm saying is—can I go ahead? Do you trust me not to back out of buying the house?'

Did she? The last two men who'd had anything to do with the manor hadn't been trustworthy at all. But this was Mike. He was different. Besides, she knew where his father lived. 'Yes,' she said.

'You're sure? Because I don't want you to hear I've got a surveyor in and be worried that I might try and beat you down on the price whilst making your house temporarily unsaleable. I only want to find out early whether any treatment is needed so I can get it sorted as soon as possible.'

'It's fine, Mike. I trust you. You can have my spare set of keys. When do you want to begin?'

'I thought tomorrow, for preference.'

Tomorrow! That really was eager! This was a

side of him she hadn't seen. Or had she? Wasn't this the same solid intractability that had got Joshua Lawrie into hospital for treatment? A pleasant, no-nonsense, velvet bulldozer?

He laughed at the look on her face. 'No point hanging around. Dad loves having us in the flat, but two men in one kitchen is a strain on any relationship. And now I need your help some more. I'd like to use local people if possible. Builders, plumbers, electricians, carpenters. You know everyone here. Can you make me a list? I realise they might not be available right now, but I would at least like to ask.'

'Of course I will. That's great, Mike, but why?'

He took a sip of his wine, his face thoughtful. 'I think it was what you said about incomers. Bethany and I are moving to Rivercut and we want to belong. And at the party I overheard one of the chaps saying he'd been laid off by a building contractor because there wasn't the work around and the company was being forced to retrench. Now, I don't know what sort of workman he is, but that man's child will be going to school with Bethany. I'd rather put bread in my daughter's friends' mouths than fill up the coffers of some big firm from Salford or wherever.'

Grace's eyes stung with tears. It was the same attitude her father had always had, but from a Londoner, a stranger… 'That's… That's…' She broke off, searching in her bag for a tissue. 'You're too good to be true.'

He looked at her seriously. 'I just want to do it right, Grace.'

She blew her nose. 'There are some people in here at this very moment who would be interested. I think you're about to make Christmas a lot brighter for a number of families. I'll introduce you and you can have a chat while I get my emotions in order.'

In fact she'd refilled her glass and had perused the menu several times before Mike rejoined her.

'Thanks,' he said, looking cheerful. 'Sorry if I took a bit long. That was really useful. I don't feel nearly so daunted now.'

'Daunted? You?' How did one daunt a steamroller?

He sat down next to her and picked up the menu. 'I'll have you know I frequently tread a fine line between bluff and counter-bluff. Mmm, home-made game pie. Wonderful. What are you having?'

It was a good meal, and by the end of it Grace felt mellow and well fed. But the pub was getting noisy and she was struggling to hear what Mike was saying.

'This is hopeless,' he mouthed. 'Shall we go?'

Grace nodded and put on her coat. Outside the Coach and Horses it was spectacularly silent. Maybe it was the change in her routine, but she felt different tonight. The cold made her tingle, not shiver. 'I don't feel as if I've drunk half a bottle of wine,' she said. 'The food must have soaked it up.'

'Same with me,' said Mike.

He stood there, perfectly at ease, gazing down the snow-covered street. Grace began to suspect that he was in no hurry for the evening to end either. She took a quick breath. Say it now and say it quickly. 'I've got a bottle of claret that was given to me by a grateful farmer. I haven't liked to drink it alone, so if you fancy another glass…'

Now he turned and looked at her steadily. 'Are you sure?' he said.

Ah, so she hadn't imagined those moments

during the meal when their arms had accidentally brushed. 'Of course I'm sure. It's just a bottle of wine after all. And you can collect the keys for the manor at the same time.' She kept the tremor out of her voice.

'So I can.' They started strolling towards her cottage. 'Why was the farmer grateful?'

Grace laughed. 'Oh, he liked the way I'd dressed the wound on his shin. He said it didn't hurt at all. All I'd done was shave the hairs on his leg before attaching the plaster.'

'Florence Nightingale would have been proud of you.'

Coloured lights shone merrily around the Christmas tree outside her door. Grace got a small pleasurable lift from the sight.

'Very handsome,' said Mike.

'Isn't it just. And there's more.' She opened her door and bent to flick the switch on at the socket. Dozens of fairy lights sprang into twinkling life on her inside tree.

'Now, that's pretty. Seems a shame to turn the main light on.'

Grace's heart beat faster. 'We don't have to. Wait a moment.'

She crossed the room to the mantelpiece, on which she had arranged two bright red candles amidst Christmas foliage. She lit them carefully and the room was changed. It became a place of shadows and magic.

Mike hung his coat on the back of the door and sat down on the settee. She could almost hear him saying, *See, I'm not looming.* Nevertheless she went rather quickly into the kitchen to fetch the wine.

The couch was big enough for two. Just. But she could feel their shoulders touching and his thigh pressed next to hers. Her hand shook just slightly as she poured the wine.

'Do you know,' he said. 'I feel really positive. I've been *doing* something this evening. Not simply my job—that's an everyday thing. Not selling my flat and selling my partnership. Those are looking-backwards things. Today I've been doing something forward-looking. Planning what needs doing to the manor. Accepting deep within myself that Bethany and I are going to live here and make a future. I've been moving on.'

Grace smiled. 'You're right. That is a good thing.' It was what she should be doing, she realised. Now the millstone of debt was gone, she should be thinking positively too. Put Peter behind her once and for all. Start to trust again. 'To the future,' she said, holding up her glass.

He clinked his against it. 'The future.' They drank in silence for a minute. 'There is one thing I'm worried about,' he continued. 'The driveway. It's so open. Anyone could walk in. Bethany could wander out. Has it always been that way?'

Oh, Mike! And there she had been thinking that with the candles and the wine, things might be approaching romantic. He was looking at her enquiringly. Grace dredged her memory. 'I'm pretty sure there used to be gates when I was small. I remember looking through openwork scrolls at the road and I can't think where else I'd have been looking if not through gates. I guess the posts rotted or something. They'll have been too big to store in the attics. You'll have to investigate the barns.'

He raised his eyebrows, amused. His blue eyes danced in the candlelight. 'They won't have been thrown away?'

'Good Lord, no. Nothing has ever been thrown away at the manor.'

He chuckled. 'If that's the case you could probably have paid several months' mortgage money out of the scrap value in the outbuildings.'

'I never thought of that.' She found herself breathing in his clean-sweater scent and a faint tang of citrus. 'You smell nice,' she murmured inconsequentially. The claret must have been more potent than the wine at the pub.

It seemed natural for him to put his arm round her shoulders. 'So do you. You feel nice too,' he replied.

An inner certainty stole over Grace, as warm and languorous as the wine. She put her glass on the table. She knew what would happen next. And she knew what might happen after that if they both let it.

She heard the 'ting' as he placed his glass on the coffee table too. And then he kissed her.

He kissed her as he'd kissed her before. Gently, tentatively almost, as if he wasn't sure what he was doing or whether he'd be welcome. But he was welcome. She trailed her fingertips down the side of his face. She could feel the slight roughness of his cheek—it had been morning when he'd shaved.

This was so easy. There was no need to hurry. She could feel his tongue exploring the insides of her lips, touching the sensitive corners of her mouth. She mirrored his actions, feeling him respond, marvelling at how right this felt. When he pulled away she felt bereft, but it was only because he'd moved on to kissing her cheeks, her forehead, even the tip of her nose. 'That's lovely,' she said.

She realised that she'd never felt quite like this before. Mike was more than just a man—he was *the* man.

Then she gasped and called out his name. Very, very gently he had nibbled the bottom of her ear. How did he know that that was one of the most sensitive parts of her body? How did he know that that combination of pleasure and the tiniest pain possible could bring her so much joy? But he did know. And he did it again. How could he know her so well?

They'd somehow moved around, turned in their embrace until they were half lying on the couch. Her head had fallen back, her body was melded tightly to his. And now he was kissing her mouth again, but this time with a growing need that was fully matched by her own. She opened up to him without restraint, giving as well as receiving, letting his tongue join hers in joyous delight.

They paused, not really wanting to stop but knowing the next step had to be taken slowly, if it was taken at all. Grace's eye fell on their two glasses. 'Do you want a drink?' she asked with a mischievous smile.

'Grace!' Then he propped himself up on one elbow. 'What have you got in mind?'

'You'll like it. Yes or no?'

'Yes. But I'd rather kiss you again.'

'Well, it involves kissing…'

She took a small sip from her glass, then raised her face to his. He kissed her. And she let the wine trickle from her mouth to his and it was more wonderful than she could have guessed.

'Oh, I like that. In fact, I think I'd like another drink—just like that one. Or would you like me to feed you some wine this time?'

The claret was warm when it arrived in her mouth, slipping over her tongue and tasting of him. Their kiss took on a momentum of its own as she ran her hands around his back, feeling his palms sweeping over the silk of her dress. She shifted, trying to indicate without words that if his hand wanted to roam lower she wouldn't object. But her leg hit the arm of the settee and her foot found the branches of the Christmas tree.

She lifted her head. 'There's not a lot of room here. Would you…? Would you like to move to somewhere more comfortable?'

For a moment the sound of his breathing was the only noise in the room. He knew as well as she did what she was asking him. What had happened so far could still be drawn back from. It could be passed off as momentary madness, perhaps to be smiled over and forgotten. But after they had gone upstairs there would be no turning back.

Huskily, he asked, 'Grace, is this really what you want?'

'Yes—if you want it too. If you don't we'll just have a lovely last kiss and then I'll put the light on and we'll finish our drinks and talk about the manor. I won't be hurt. I won't be offended.'

'I do want it,' he muttered. 'Part of my head is telling me to walk away, but most of me thinks you are gorgeous and generous and intelligent and I would like very much indeed to make love to you.'

He'd said it. It was out in the open. Grace's whole body quivered. 'Come on, then,' she whispered, and took his hand to lead him up the narrow stairs.

Upstairs she switched on her bedside reading lamp and pulled the curtains. Mike held her hand again as he sat on the edge of the double bed and looked around at the small items of furniture she'd brought from the manor, at the faded duvet and matching curtains that had been hers for years, at the pictures—as many as the room would hold.

'Thank you,' he said softly, squeezing her hand. 'Thank you for trusting me enough to bring me up here. This is a very special room for you, isn't it?'

Grace felt her eyes sting again. He was right. And because he had sensed what her bedroom meant to her, she knew everything from now on would be fine.

'Yes,' she said simply.

He smiled, his face gentle in the shadows. 'Come here and lie down next to me. Just for the moment I'd like to kiss you without getting a crick in my neck.'

So they slipped off their shoes and lay side by side on the duvet. Mike eased his arm under her head and she rolled gladly towards him, her knee bending naturally so that her leg was half on top of his. As they kissed, his hands unhurriedly roamed her body, feeling the pulse in her neck, stroking her back, cupping the edge of her breast.

This was good, simply relaxing and getting to know his body, enjoying the shivers of pleasure as he got to know hers. And all the time something was building inside both of them—the urge to move on, to take this new, tentative delight to greater heights.

His fingers ran down the indentation of her spine, curved over her hips, found the hem of her dress. And then up her nylon-clad leg until…

'Stockings,' he said, his voice breaking. 'Oh, Grace, do you know what you do to a man?'

'I can take them off if you like,' she said, a laugh in her voice.

'Don't you dare.' He brushed the bare skin and moved on up underneath the blue silk. He found the lacy cup of her bra, lingered for an exquisite moment then slid around the back to the fastening. A moment later it was undone. Grace felt her whole self trembling as his hand moved back to cover her breast.

'Oh, Mike,' she breathed, and rolled onto her back, lifting her arms in mute invitation for him to ease her dress up and off. She heard his intake of breath, his inarticulate gasp of pleasure.

The bra came off with the dress. He leaned over her upper body, slowly stroking from the shoulders down and around each curve. Grace felt the skin of her breasts tighten, her nipples harden in anticipation. He brushed them with his palms, rubbed with his fingers—but so slowly!

'Mike…please…' she murmured, aching for more.

At last his head bowed over her and his tongue touched first one then the second proud peak. She moaned—then cried out with delight as he took one into his mouth. That was so good!

She reached out, wanting to touch him too. Her fingers encountered fine Shetland wool. Her eyes flew open. 'Mike, you're still dressed!'

'Mmm? Oh, so I am.'

Grace snatched her dressing gown from the bedpost, pulling it around her. 'Just to make us even,' she said at his protest. 'Stand up—I want to do this properly.' She slid off the bed to face him. First his sweater joined her dress on the floor. Then she undid all his shirt buttons and slid it off. He had a magnificent torso. She spent a moment admiring it before running her hands lightly down his front to his belt. It was a matter of seconds before he was stepping out of his jeans, but when she gripped the waistband of his black silk boxers he put his hands over hers.

'Aren't we forgetting something?' he said. 'We're not even any more.'

Grace's insides turned to liquid. She raised one foot and rested it on the bed so he could peel off the stocking. Then did the same with the other. She loosened the belt of her dressing gown but just as the front was about to part she put a hand to her mouth. 'Oh,' she said, suddenly remembering something. 'Mike, it is Christmas, you know.'

'I do know. Why do you mention it?'

'Because last weekend my six-year-old god-daughter gave me a very silly present that she had picked out herself and made me promise to wear to my first Christmas party of the season.'

'Which was today.'

'Er, yes.'

'Okay, I'm warned.' He untied her belt and pushed the dressing gown off her shoulders to fall in a soft heap on the carpet. He looked down—and a smile crossed his face.

'I'll have you know they're very warm and comfortable,' she said.

'I still want to take them off you.' And then he laughed joyously. 'I'll bet no one at that party today guessed that underneath your gorgeous slinky dress you were wearing a pair of white satin knickers with happy Father Christmases all over them.'

Delicately he slid the white satin downwards, his hands lingering on her skin. Delicately she did the same for him, feeling the first thrilling touch of his warm maleness against her abdomen. With one hand she pulled back the duvet.

He swore.

'Mike?' What had she done?

He growled in frustration. 'I…I didn't expect… It's been such a long time since…'

She giggled. 'I've got a box of condoms in my bedside drawer. I was going to throw them out when…' She broke off. 'But I never got round to it.' She looked up at him shyly. 'I'm glad now.'

Mike took her in his arms and swept her off her feet and into the bed. 'So am I.'

It was different now when she felt him beside her, both of them lying down between her sheets. For a moment there had been a respite, time for a joke even. She realised that she had been more nervous than she knew. But now they were in bed together, they were naked and the delight she had felt before returned, but heightened so much.

He pulled her close to him. Kissing him was even more wonderful now. Not only their lips but their entire bodies were touching. She could feel the warmth, the softness of his skin pressed against hers. Her breasts, the peaks stiff and unbearably sensitive, were crushed against the muscles of his chest. Her smooth legs rubbed against the faint roughness of his. And pressed hard against her thigh was the indisputable sign of his need for her.

Every kiss, every touch told her that she wanted him, needed him with an urgency she had never experienced before. She had met this man only a few days before but now it seemed she had known him for ever. It was as if their coming together had been ordained since that first encounter.

She could tell he shared her frantic need. This would not, could not last long. One more searing kiss and she rolled onto her back, pulling him until he was poised above her. 'Grace… Grace… I…'

'Don't talk. There's no need. Make me complete, Mike.' Her arms encircled his neck, she urged him down onto her. Into her. She cried out at the same time as he gasped.

'Oh, Mike.'

'Oh, Grace.'

It was good, more than good. She was taking him, but giving to him. He was taking her, and giving to her. They were in perfect unison.

No use now trying to wait, to tease, to pretend that they had all the time in the world. Together they moved towards a climax, an ending that had them both gripping each other and calling out in ecstasy.

He collapsed on her, holding her tight, and kissed her again and again. 'Oh, Grace.'

'Shh. That was lovely. Shh.'

They lay side by side, curled into one another, their arms across each other's bodies, drifting into sleep. But always there was that consciousness of his arms round her, his body next to hers. She was content. She was complete. She was happy.

It was dark, Mike was warm and in his half waking, half sleeping state he was aware of burgeoning love and great fulfilment. Something had been missing for such a long time—a part of him ripped away and only an aching gap left in its place. But here, now, he was whole again. There was regular breathing in the darkness, drifting hair tickling his cheek. He reached out and his hand slipped over warm, smooth skin. 'Oh, Sarah,' he murmured.

Sarah. Grace lay curled up on her side, tucked into Mike's warm body, his arm loosely around her. Her eyes were shut, her limbs relaxed. Only the tear trickling down her cheek as her lover spoke his dead wife's name showed that she was awake.

CHAPTER NINE

MIKE came awake properly. For a split second he was surprised beyond belief to find a woman in his arms. But memory flooded back—and what a memory! He kissed Grace's neck softly. 'Grace, I have to leave. I can't not be at home when Bethany wakes up in the morning.'

She stirred, twisted to face him, pushing her hair out of the way. Lord, she was gorgeous. Her breasts rubbed against his chest, bringing a resurgence of desire. 'Are you going?' she said sleepily.

'I must.' He kissed her eyelids, pausing at the taste of salt. 'Have you been crying?'

'Yes… No… That was lovely, Mike.'

'It was. Don't get up, it's too cold. I'll see you tomorrow—today—whenever it is. Come and have a picnic lunch with us again.'

She padded downstairs anyway, wrapped in her dressing gown, to bolt the door after him.

That last view of her, tousled and beautiful, stayed with him as he strode up the high street through cold, crunching snow under a waning moon. Something to keep him warm.

But as he opened the door to the flat he heard Bethany's rising wail. 'Daddy! I want my daddy!'

He tore off his coat as he raced to her room. 'I'm here, sweetheart. What's the matter?' He scooped his daughter up, feeling his heart thud as he cradled her to his chest. She was limp. He peered anxiously at her face in the light from the hallway. Was she flushed? Sweating? How long had she been crying?

She gave a small murmur and turned to snuggle into his sweater. False alarm. She was still asleep. Thank God. He held her a moment longer—then very gently slid her back into bed, testing her forehead to be on the safe side, lifting her wrist to check her pulse.

'Everything all right?' asked his father from the doorway.

For a moment Mike felt a quite shattering anger. Bethany had cried out and James hadn't been instantly with her. He'd trusted him to look after her. But then he had a vision of himself in

Grace's arms, oblivious to the rest of the world. He was the one to blame, not his father.

'Talking in her sleep,' he said in a low voice. 'Nothing to worry about.' He followed James out of the room and pulled the door to.

'Good evening?' said his father.

'The best.' But he felt a small core of misery settle in his chest. He couldn't do it again. Bethany had needed him tonight and he hadn't been there. He wouldn't risk that happening any more.

Sarah. No matter how many times Grace replayed the events of the evening, she couldn't get that one word out of her head. He had said it in that moment between sleeping and waking, said it when the rigid guard on his memories was lulled. She had to face it. Whatever she had been beginning to believe, whatever hopes she had allowed to come into existence, the fact was that Mike still mourned his wife. He was still in love with Sarah.

Which left her where? Friends with him? Just friends after what they had shared? The idea was laughable.

Grace was clear-sighted enough to recognise

that she had been in need of their lovemaking tonight just as much as Mike. He hadn't had any intention of taking her for granted or making a fool of her. Maybe he had no idea himself how much of his heart was still Sarah's.

So…she would be there to talk to, there to listen to him. And, God help her, she would be there to satisfy that other need if loneliness overtook them again. But it was a hell of a way to live.

As it happened, she couldn't make it to the surgery for lunch the next day. One of her outlying patients needed stitches removed. Another had an appointment with a home care visitor and Grace had been asked if she could be present. She sent Mike a friendly text to explain. As she drove through the snowy hills, she reflected that it was probably just as well. The less she saw him physically, the easier it would be to keep a mental distance. Kinder for both of them. Less heart-breaking.

She was surprised by one thing: the estate agent phoned to tell her he'd had another offer for the manor *above* the original asking price.

'It's too late,' she said. 'I'm selling the house to Dr Curtis.'

The agent pointed out that the contract had yet to be signed. Grace replied that the formal offer had been accepted and that she didn't go back on her word. Odd, she thought, but put it out of her mind.

It didn't take too much effort to be busy the following day as well, but she was conscious that she had promised to take Bethany to her riding lesson. Subtle questioning of the surgery receptionist elicited the information that young Dr Curtis would be out all afternoon. Grace asked her to relay the message that she would pick up Bethany's riding clothes from his room at two-thirty.

There were vans in the driveway of the manor as she went past. She drove resolutely on, ignoring a sharp stab of pain. Mike was buying the manor from her. He would make it beautiful again, a proper home for himself and Bethany. But seeing workmen there, she finally realised that what once had been a much-loved haven was lost to her for ever. She let herself into the surgery as near desolation as she had been in a long time.

She paused on the threshold of Mike's room. He had put his stamp on it already. He'd shifted the computer onto his desk and moved the desk nearer to the window. There was the same tang of citrus in the room that she'd smelled on his skin on Tuesday night.

She mustn't think about that. Not go there. Where were Bethany's clothes? Ah, in a bag on the desk. She reached for them quickly—and was arrested by the sight of a framed photo.

It was large, ten inches by eight, and it showed a laughing family. There was Mike, his head thrown back and a wide smile splitting his face. He looked younger, carefree, happy. And there was Bethany balanced on her father's hip, dark curls dancing, giggling as if she would never stop. And there…there was Sarah. Also laughing, her head tipped towards Mike so that they framed their daughter.

Grace sat down numbly, unable to take her eyes off the photo. No wonder Mike was still in love with Sarah. She was an adult version of Bethany. Every time Mike looked at his daughter he must see his wife's face. How could any woman compete with that?

There was a note on the desk. *'Grace—busy this afternoon. Can you bring Bethany back, please? Thanks. Mike X'*

X. A kiss. Grace remembered his real kisses,

pressed into her skin, taking her to such places of delight. She looked at the photo again. Even if they made a go of this, even if she let herself trust again, she would always be second best.

Lorna Threlkeld was just getting into her car as Grace and Bethany arrived at Rivercut Stables. She stopped, waiting for them, her face set in sour lines. 'Bethany Curtis, isn't it?'

'That's right,' said Grace. 'She enjoyed last week's lesson.'

'The little girl whose father is buying the manor. How very convenient, Grace.'

Grace's chin came up. 'It's convenient for Bethany because she won't have so far to walk to school.'

'And convenient for you too,' said Lorna with a malevolent look.

Grace knew perfectly well what the other woman was insinuating, but she kept her voice pleasant. 'It's certainly nice to have found a buyer at the right price,' she said, holding Bethany's hand somewhat tighter. 'We mustn't miss Bethany's lesson. Goodbye.'

A nasty little interlude, but as they walked on,

a sudden amusing thought struck Grace. Could it have been Lorna's father who had put in that cut-price offer for the manor some time ago? Yes, she could just see him wanting to add it to his other properties in the area and turning it into holiday apartments or a country house hotel. He'd probably been holding back until she was desperate to sell at any price. But Lorna must have driven through the village and noticed the comings and goings so he had hurriedly contacted the estate agent and raised his bid. Ha! Too late, Mr Threlkeld. That will teach you to be greedy.

Her phone bleeped part way through the lesson. At the next pause, Grace looked at the text. 'It's from Daddy,' she said to Bethany. 'He wants us to call at the manor on the way back. He says he's found something exciting.'

'Treasure!' said Bethany straight away.

'I wish,' replied Grace. Sadly, knowing Mike, it was probably the old driveway gates so he could keep Bethany safe and sound and fenced off from the world.

They parked next to Mike's Range Rover. There were another couple of cars there too. Bethany danced in through the front door. It was a good thing it was open, thought Grace, it would have felt really weird using the knocker to her own home.

And there was Mike in conversation with a builder from the village, glancing towards the door and breaking into a smile. Grace stopped with an almost physical blow. So much for increasing mental distance. Just seeing him brought it all back. How could she have forgotten how wonderful he looked?

'Did you have a good lesson, sweetheart?' he said, lifting Bethany in his arms. He kissed her, but his eyes were on Grace. 'Hi, Grace. How have you been?'

She had to keep up the pretence. Everything between them must appear unchanged. 'Oh, busy as usual. I might need your advice on one of today's calls.'

He was instantly alert. 'Serious?'

She shook her head. 'No. But a visit sooner rather than later would be good.'

Bethany was wriggling. 'Where's the treasure, Daddy?'

He laughed. 'It's not treasure, darling. It's a thing. What do you know about this, Grace?'

Such a strange exchange. The last time they

had seen each other had been in her bedroom. They had just… It had been one of the most marvellous experiences of her life. And now they were casually chatting about patients and houses. Grace knew it was how she'd wanted it, but even so it took some getting used to.

Mike put Bethany down and led the way over to the fireplace. Grace saw with a jolt that it had been unblocked. She hoped he could afford the fuel bills that would be needed to combat the draughts.

Then she looked at the hall properly and was amazed. Mike had had the oak panelling cleaned. What a strange place to start! Surely there were more pressing aspects to be sorted out? But he was looking at her expectantly, his hand on an area of panel to the left of the fireplace.

'Ta-da!' he said, and pressed on the panelling. A black oblong appeared behind it.

'The secret passage!' exclaimed Grace, utterly delighted. Memories crowded back. She rushed to put them into words. 'To be exact, the secret entrance. When I was a little girl I thought it very Enid Blyton. Secrets in a house! There was a doorway here that led into a kind of long alcove at one end of the kitchen. It meant servants in the old days could serve drinks and food in the hall without having to walk all the way around through the corridors. But when the door was shut it just looked like the rest of the panelling. We didn't have servants so my father had the doorway bricked up and a big fridge-freezer installed in the alcove instead.'

'That explains it. We found it when we were cleaning the panelling. I couldn't resist trying to discover where it went so we knocked the bricks out and then pushed the fridge-freezer out of the way at the other end.' He grinned. 'Must say, I felt a bit Enid Blyton myself. Do you want to walk through? Revisit your childhood?'

'I do,' said Bethany, tugging his hand. 'Open the secret door, Daddy.'

'Careful of the brick rubble,' he said. 'Grace?'

There was an infectious excitement in his face. Grace felt herself melt. 'I'd love to.'

He eased the panelling door open. Bethany was instantly through it. Grace followed Mike more slowly. The arched passage was shorter than she remembered, the air hazy with brick dust and the tiled floor gritty underfoot. But it was magic. Mike was right—it was childhood revisited.

In front of them Bethany was already squealing with delight at having come out in a whole different room. Mike looked over his shoulder at Grace, his eyes brimming with amusement as he reached to clasp her hand. 'Fun?' he said.

His hand was strong and vital and alive. His joy in this simple thing was overwhelming. For a moment she was too full of emotion to speak. This was the man he was supposed to be. She settled for nodding. 'Fun.'

And she knew, here and now, permanently and for ever, that she loved him.

'Again,' shouted Bethany, running from the kitchen past Grace back to the hall. Mike jogged after her.

Grace remained in the kitchen, where they both joined her a few moments later.

'I'll have the alcove swept and cleaned and painted,' said Mike, panting slightly as he caught his over-excited daughter. 'And I'll have the secret door oiled. The passage is going to be so useful to get to and from the kitchen. Oh—and I got hold of a firm that refurbishes old ranges. And then later on I'd like a conservatory built onto the end wall there. It'll be a real living kitchen.'

'It sounds—it sounds lovely, Mike. I think you're going to be really happy here.'

He caught his breath. 'I hope so.'

'So who's this patient you were worried about?'

Grace looked up in surprise. She'd been immersed in writing up the morning's notes and hadn't heard Mike come into her room. She was even more surprised when he put a mug of tea on the desk in front of her.

'Peace offering in advance,' he said. 'I need to drag you down to the solicitor so we can sign a notice of intent of buy and I can pay you a deposit. Someone's been leaning on the estate agent—this should settle their hash.'

'Lorna Threlkeld's father!' exclaimed Grace wrathfully. 'I'll be glad to sign anything you like. But there's no need to pay me yet.'

'You don't have Christmas presents to buy? Besides, the money's better in your account than theirs.'

'If you insist, then.' She got the feeling that refusal would be futile at any time, but especially today. There was something different about Mike. He was edgy, his voice held an underlying tension.

Had the surveyor uncovered something wrong with the manor? She kept her voice cheerful. 'And, yes, I always need to get more presents. I'm having a day's shopping in Manchester with Natalie tomorrow. It'll be nice to know there are funds to cover the credit-card bill.'

His face lightened. 'Natalie? The girl you trained with? The one whose daughter has such exceptional taste in underwear?'

Grace's heart skipped a beat at this reminder of the other night. 'That's her. But you'll be glad to hear Chloe is having a daddy day, so we'll be alone this time.' What was she saying? She'd intimated there might be another bedroom occasion! 'Always assuming we get out of the café, that is,' she said hurriedly. 'Put two friends together with unlimited coffee and we might just talk all day instead.'

'But that's good too. It's always good to have a friend.'

Oh, dear, was he reflecting that he'd left all his friends in London? She couldn't seem to say anything right. Then she remembered why he'd come into her room in the first place. Talking about work was safe. 'That patient I mentioned.

Mrs King.' She brought up the file on the computer, shifting so Mike could read it.

He pulled across a chair and studied the screen. Suddenly he was a doctor, a professional, not just Mike. 'Ivy King,' he murmured. 'Seventy-five years old with high blood pressure. What's the problem?'

'I called in to do her regular check-up. All seemed normal, the diastolic pressure was slightly up, but nothing to worry about. Then her daughter mentioned that Ivy had had several falls recently. It's not like her.'

'Did she appear weaker? Slurred speech?'

Grace made a helpless gesture. 'A bit more frail. I just…'

'You're wondering whether they were transient ischaemic attacks? Grace, it's not the end of the world if they were.'

Grace nodded, but still felt worried. A TIA happened when a small piece of fatty material came away from the wall of an artery, was transported to the brain and caused a temporary blockage. They were often the result of high blood pressure and they tended to grow more frequent with age. Recovery was usually quite quick. The danger was that in time the underlying cause might lead to a stroke.

'I'd still appreciate you doing a proper examination.'

'Then I will. Do you want to call in after we've seen the solicitor?'

Grace glanced at the clock on the wall. 'Will you have time before collecting Bethany from school?'

'She's going to a friend's house for tea. I've been instructed to pick her up at six o'clock.'

'Then, yes, please. Can you give me twenty minutes to get these notes finished?'

'Sure. I'll go and read up properly on Mrs King.'

It was all quite straightforward at the solicitor's office. Grace signed and was witnessed, signed again and was witnessed again. In a tone decrying his bad taste for mentioning it, the solicitor murmured that Mike's deposit would go straight into Grace's bank account. Grace said cheerfully that her bank manager would probably go out and get quietly drunk.

That almost brought a smile to Mike's lips, and when he was examining Mrs King he seemed normal too, if slightly withdrawn. But after he had suggested gently to Ivy that he arrange a trip to hospital for her for further tests, and they consulted a calendar to fix on the best time, Grace saw a shutter come over his face. Instinctively she took over the conversation, chatting in a friendly way as they moved to the door.

'So,' she finished, 'you're not to worry, Ivy. We just want to be on the safe side.'

'All right, young Grace,' said Ivy King. 'As long as the tests don't interfere with my Christmas, I'll go quietly. Run along now. Dr Curtis will be wanting to pick up his little girl. Bonny little thing she is, by what people say. Oh, and we're all pleased as punch that you're taking over the manor, Doctor. And there's not one of us believe the gossip neither.'

'Gossip?' said Mike when they were eventually in his car again. 'Which gossip would that be?'

Grace felt her cheeks heat. 'Nothing that matters.'

He looked at her as if he didn't believe her.

'Drive,' she said. 'You can tell me something soothing about how much you're having to pay to refurbish the central heating as we go. I saw the plumber's van turn up this morning as I was leaving for work. I can't believe you've found a system that will actually keep the main hall warm in winter.'

He gave her another of those piercing looks, but talked amiably enough until they came to a halt behind a line of traffic.

Grace peered ahead. It was obvious what had happened. A wedge of snow had slid suddenly down onto the road, causing a car to veer off. It didn't look as if anyone was hurt, but the road was blocked by the recovery lorry. Grace was used to this sort of scenario. She got Mrs King's case notes out of her case to annotate them. Mike, however, sat tensely, his eyes on the lorry, tapping the steering-wheel and casting harried glances at the dashboard clock.

'Why did this have to happen today?' he muttered. 'If I knew the roads around here I could take a back route home.'

Grace looked up. 'Mike, I know the roads and there aren't any back routes. Who is Bethany having tea with? Give her mother a ring. She'll understand. Or ask James to collect her if you're really worried about her outstaying her welcome.'

'I can't. He's going out for the whole evening.'

'Then ring,' she advised placidly. 'It'll be fine. We're used to unexpected snow-dumps in this part of the country during the winter.'

Bethany, predictably, was not in the least alarmed at Mike turning up late. She'd had a lovely time and was delighted to see Grace in the car too. But back at the surgery she set up a wail when she realised Grace was unlocking her Land Rover instead of coming indoors.

'I want Grace to stay!'

'Grace has things to do. It's nearly Christmas and she has to—'

'But I want to show her the bath toys Grandad gave me!' Tears started to roll down Bethany's cheeks.

Mike glanced at Grace, who nodded her head. 'All right, Bethany, just this once because it's nearly Christmas. But then you go straight to bed and be good!'

'All right,' said Bethany, demure now she had got her own way.

In fact, she was very tired after the excitement of playing with her friend. Bathtime was soon over and teeth cleaned. Grace offered to read a story, but the little girl was asleep before she reached the end of the first page. Grace looked down at her, wondering if this was how Sarah had looked in sleep. She withdrew quietly to the living room.

Mike was sitting staring into the fire, legs stretched out in front of him, his head resting on his hand. Grace saw his expression before he realised she was there. He looked sad, something she hadn't seen before. She wondered what he was thinking.

'Bethany's worn out,' she reported. 'It must be terribly tiring being a sociable five-year-old.'

He stirred. 'Thanks for putting her to bed. I don't usually pander to her but…' He broke off. 'Are you hungry at all? I was thinking of warming up some soup. And maybe a glass of wine?'

Grace remembered the last glass of wine they'd drunk together. She smiled—about to make an allusive remark—but realised with a slight shock and just a tiny touch of pique that sex wasn't on Mike's mind at all. But something was. Something that had brought a grey look to his face and defeat to his voice. 'That would be nice,' she said neutrally. 'Shall I help? Where is it all?'

He started to get up—almost had to drag himself. 'Sorry, I'm not being much of a host.'

Then Grace remembered something he had said earlier. *It's always good to have a friend.* 'Mike, tell me if I'm wrong, but is now one of those times when you'd like a friend?' she asked.

'Sorry?'

'There's something troubling you, it's obvious. And earlier you said that it was always good to have a friend. Well, I'm here and I'm a friend. What's the problem?'

He laughed shortly. 'Ten out of ten for observation skills. Yes, there is something bothering me, but it's not a problem. It's an anniversary.'

'Anniversary? Of what?'

Another silence, and then he said, 'I've been trying to forget it all day. Today my wife would have been thirty. But there'll be no party.'

'And it hurts.'

'It hurts. Last year her birthday was sheer agony, coming so soon after…after the accident. I thought this year it might be easier. And I suppose it is. A bit.' He frowned. 'Grace, this isn't the kind of thing I should be talking to you about. We've got very close and—'

'Mike, I want you to talk! You loved her, and I…I think that's great. So tell me about her, tell me about her birthdays.'

He laughed, and this time Grace thought there might be some genuine humour. 'I can take them or leave them but Sarah was like Bethany. She was so serious and intent for most of the time, but she loved birthdays and birthday parties. We always went to a bit of trouble for her. Two years ago I took her and Bethany on the London Eye at night. As it went round we had a picnic out of the rucksack I'd packed. Then I told her to close her eyes, and Bethany and I gave her her birthday cake.'

'A birthday cake? In a rucksack?'

Mike almost smiled. 'Two birthday cakes. Two little iced cakes, one with two candles on, one with eight. Because she was twenty-eight.'

'That sounds magic.' Grace couldn't help herself. She took his hand. 'Tell me what Sarah was like,' she said. 'It might be painful but it might help. I think it's wrong to try to forget, it's better to remember—to remember the good times, remember how much they outweighed the bad. Describe her to me.'

For a moment she thought he was going to

refuse, but then he took a deep breath. 'She was a very slim woman, athletic but not as tall as you. She had a young face, sort of pointed—elfin some people called it. Dark hair, wavy like Bethany's. She had big dark eyes, dark green, and a piercing look. Sometimes she'd stay silent and just look at you so you wanted desperately to say something to her.'

'And she was a doctor, like you.'

'Yes. She never believed that some problems are insoluble, are beyond a doctor's abilities. She got involved when she shouldn't and when she failed it hurt her.'

'That's a good fault, don't you think? Better than the opposite.'

'True. You remind me of her that way sometimes.'

Grace felt like crying. 'Thank you, that's a lovely thing to say. I can see why you miss her.'

'I do. Sometimes I think I always will.' He buried his face in his hands. 'And sometimes I resent that. How can that be? How can I resent Sarah? I loved her. I loved her so much.'

Grace watched, alarmed now, as he crouched forward, his hands gripped together. 'Grief doesn't follow normal rules, Mike. Love alters us. Maybe…maybe our bodies can't cope immediately. Maybe when the one we love has gone, our bodies try to snap back to how they were before. But they can't. I think…I think the thing to do is to move on, but remember the past.'

'Easier said than done. Do you still want some soup?'

She followed him into the kitchen where he took a large bowl of home-made chowder out of the fridge and ladled it into a saucepan. There were crusty rolls to go with it, and half a bottle of red wine. He brushed against her as he reached for his glass. His wedding ring knocked her knuckle. Mike studied his hand for a long moment before carrying the food through to the other room.

This time the conversation was easier. They talked about some tiny changes Mike wanted to make to the practice, but wasn't sure whether his father would agree with. By the end of the simple meal, Grace thought Mike was probably all right again. She was glad she'd been here—as a friend—when he'd hit that low point.

'I'd better go,' she said. 'I'll leave the car here

and walk. Don't want to risk running over any stray carol singers when I've had a drink.'

'Wait a minute.' Mike sat upright, his voice strained. Grace realised she had been premature in thinking him over his earlier emotion.

He spread his hands out, looked at the left one. 'I remember the time in church, getting married, when we exchanged rings. For me it was the happiest moment of the ceremony. They didn't match, our rings. I gave Sarah one I'd had specially made—in white gold. She didn't have much money of her own, so she gave me her grandmother's ring, enlarged to fit my finger. That's why it's so narrow. She joked that when she was a world-famous consultant she'd have a broader one made for me. I said I didn't want one. I just wanted this one, given to me with love.'

'That's lovely,' whispered Grace, tears in her eyes.

'Sarah's ring was ruined in the fire in the crash. This one…' He pulled at the narrow band on the third finger of his left hand.

Grace couldn't help herself. 'No, don't! It's a symbol, it reminds you that—'

'I need to look forward,' he said fiercely. He

tugged the ring off his finger at last, kissed it then put it on the table. 'I shan't wear it again.'

This was wrong. This was so wrong. There were tears in his eyes and Grace couldn't bear it. She gave it a moment then asked, 'So do you feel different now? More comfortable? A new person?'

'No.' There was a world of pain in his answer.

Grace picked up the ring from the table, lifted Mike's hand from where it lay desolately in his lap and slipped Sarah's wedding band back onto his finger. 'You loved her, she loved you and she'll always be part of you. Don't fight it, Mike. Accept it. Go forward with her behind you, urging you on.'

She stood up. He stood too, slightly dazed, at a loss. Grace put her arms round him and hugged him tightly. 'You'll be all right,' she said, and kissed his cheek. 'But if you need a friend, phone me.'

It took a great, great effort of will to shrug into her coat and leave the house. But she had to. Because otherwise she might have said those fatal words, words Mike wasn't anywhere near ready to hear. She said them outside, though. Closed the door firmly behind her and then looked back at the solid wood panel.

'Sleep well, Mike,' she whispered. 'I love you.'

CHAPTER TEN

THERE was another snowfall that night but in the morning the sun was out and the light on the white moors was beautiful. No one could be unhappy on a day like this, thought Grace as she drove out of Rivercut and the full beauty of the landscape hit her. She had a brief moment of regret for her old bedroom at the manor—she'd have seen this view as soon as she pulled her curtains.

No. She set her thoughts resolutely towards lively, bustling Manchester and the day of Christmas shopping awaiting her. The manor belonged to Mike now. The view would most likely be Bethany's. She must be content with her small cottage and rejoice in the simple fact that she could now afford to pay the rent *and* have money left over for more than just the basics of life.

Mike. All the curtains had been drawn still

when she'd picked up her car. She hoped he'd got some sleep last night, not stayed up wrestling with his memories. She hadn't had a phone call. That was a good sign, wasn't it?

In Manchester she met up with Natalie, who needed a posh outfit for a charity do on New Year's Eve. With a pleasurable thrill, Grace realised that she would not be restricted to merely admiring her friend—she could dress up too!

An entire morning later, Natalie was the possessor of a strapless number in dark red satin—and Grace had blown an awful lot of salary on a full-length gold taffeta gown with diamanté spaghetti straps and a seductive slit from thigh to ankle. She didn't give a thought to when she would actually wear such a dress. Whenever the occasion arose, she'd be ready! On the way out of the store they stopped in the children's clothes department. Grace was charmed to see full-length party dresses for little girls. 'I'll get one for Bethany,' she said aloud.

'Pardon?' asked her friend.

'Bethany Curtis. Mike's daughter. I told them how I used to walk down the staircase at home holding a long skirt above my ankles just like a film star. Bethany would love to do that. And I know she doesn't have any long dresses. This can be her Christmas present.'

'Good idea,' said Natalie. 'I'll buy one for Chloe too. How old did you say Bethany was?' And she continued to ask casual questions about Bethany and Mike as they looked through the racks.

It was when they were having lunch at a chic city restaurant that Grace felt a tap on her shoulder. 'Grace Fellowes! Haven't seen you for ages! And Natalie Wright too. What a sight for sore eyes.'

Grace swung round. It was Dr Robert Ross, a friend that she and Natalie had worked with some years before. He now held a senior position in a hospital in Manchester. And it seemed he was looking for staff. He joined them for coffee and told them about it.

'Half the time teaching—sharing your practical knowledge—the rest of the time proper hands-on nursing. Think about it, Grace. You've been a rural nurse for quite long enough. It's time your talents were recognised. There's more money in it.'

More money. Three weeks ago, those two

words would have made Grace seriously consider the proposition. Now she laughed. 'Thanks, Robert, but inner-city nursing—even hospital nursing with all the up-to-date equipment—it's just not for me.'

'But you're wasting away out there in the sticks! Look around you—don't you deserve this?'

'Right here, right now, it's tempting. As soon as I get home I'll wonder what you spiked my coffee with.'

The afternoon was spent in more shopping. There were several people in the village Grace needed to get small presents for, but all the time she was conscious she hadn't bought anything for Mike. But what? What did you get for the man who was buying your house—a house that needed a considerable amount of work doing to it—at a far too reasonable price? What did you get for the man who had been your lover for a few glorious hours one magical evening?

'Penny for them?' said Natalie. She had the air of having said it before.

'Oh, sorry. I was trying to remember what else I wanted.'

Natalie looked smug. 'I just need the an-tiquarian bookshop. Perhaps you'll be struck by inspiration there.'

And perhaps not. She didn't even know what Mike liked to read.

At the shop, Natalie plunged into discussion with the bookseller to whom she had already emailed her husband's wish list. Grace riffled idly through a stack of framed maps and prints—and stopped, amazed. There was an old hand-coloured map of Rivercut Village and the farms around it! She knew instantly that it would be the perfect present for Mike. It was the whole area the practice covered. It even had the manor inscribed in the centre! She blinked a bit at the price but the shopkeeper, in a fit of generosity brought on by Natalie's lavish squandering of her husband's money, reduced the amount by a third.

'That's lovely,' said Natalie. 'Where are you going to hang it?'

'I'm not,' said Grace absently. 'It's for Mike.'

Natalie pounced. 'Aha! I knew it! When do we get to meet him? Remember, you always promised I could be your matron of honour!'

'It's not like that.'

But the trouble with friends who knew you rather well was that they didn't believe the 'just good friends' line for a minute. 'Grace, you've been talking about him all day.'

'I have not!'

'Well, he's made a lot more appearances in your conversation than anyone else has.' Natalie's voice warmed; she clasped her friend's hand. 'He sounds nice.'

'He is.'

'So what's the problem? Not still that jerk Peter, is it?'

Grace sighed. 'In a way. Partly. It's quite difficult to trust after something like that. But it's also Mike. I told you his wife died in a car crash last year. Well…he's still in love with her.'

Natalie looked at her solemnly. 'But you have slept with him, right?'

'Natalie!'

'Grace, you're acting sad, but your eyes light up when you mention him.'

'That doesn't come into it. I don't…' She paused, realising it was true. 'I don't want to be second best.'

* * *

It seemed a very long journey back. Leaving the bright lights of Manchester, leaving the shops and restaurants and wide streets and bold sculptures and bustling activity. But the moors soothed Grace as always, even ghostly white and deserted in the darkness. And coming into Rivercut's narrow main road with the Carters' over-the-top Christmas display visible from the edge of the village, she smiled, wondering how she could have been so daft to consider Robert's offer even for a moment.

The Carters had competition—the manor was ablaze with lights, several vans parked in the drive. Grace was impressed. Mike had meant it when he'd said he wanted to get started on necessary work as soon as possible. Part of her wanted to pull into the drive, to see what it was he was doing. But part of her preferred to leave well alone, to remember the manor as it had always been, decaying grandeur and all. All the same, curiosity might have won if her car headlights hadn't suddenly caught the glint of wrought-iron gates. A pattern of graceful loops and whorls she hadn't seen since childhood.

Grace rolled numbly to a halt, unable to look

away. Mike must have found the gates in one of the barns. Not only found them—he'd had gateposts installed and fixed them back in place. She wound down her window to the acrid smell of new paint.

Gates across the drive again. No matter that they were standing open now, the very fact of them being there at all proclaimed the change in ownership. The manor was no longer her home.

Mike was woken up by a heavy weight clambering on top of him. For a split second his sleepy body hoped it might be Grace, but the words 'Daddy! Daddy!' made him realise his mistake.

'Go away,' he grumbled. 'It's Sunday.'

His daughter giggled. 'I know.'

He growled and caught her in a tickling cuddle. It was only later, washed, dressed and breakfasted, holding Bethany's hand as she skipped beside him on their way to the manor, that Mike realised his first thought that morning had been for Grace, not Sarah. The revelation came as such a shock that he missed his footing and thumped down hard in a sitting position, half in snow, half in slush. Bethany found it highly amusing.

'If you're tired you should have knocked,'

called a voice. 'You could have rested for a moment before going on to the manor.'

Grace! She was just putting her bag into the Land Rover. Mike scrambled to his feet, brushing snow off his anorak. She looked gorgeous. Wait a moment, though… 'Why are you in uniform?' he said with a frown. 'It's Sunday.'

'One of my patients had a fall overnight and the dressing is oozing.'

'But you're off duty. Can't they ring the out-of-hours service?'

'Mike, it'll take me forty minutes maximum. Don't fuss.'

Don't fuss? He was a doctor! It was his job to fuss. 'Grace, I've seen too many medical professionals have breakdowns because they do too much. You have to look after yourself. Time off—time spent doing things for yourself—is important.'

She smiled and opened the driver's door. 'All I had planned for this morning was wrapping presents. How can that be more important than a patient in pain?'

There was no answer to that. Mike felt all the frustration of arguing with a woman who knew she was in the right. 'Just you make sure it is only forty minutes, then,' he said grumpily.

'It will be.'

'We've got presents,' said Bethany, fixing on the important bit of the conversation. 'Under Grandad's tree.' She sighed. 'But I'm not allowed to open them until Christmas.'

'Fair's fair,' said Grace. 'Baby Jesus had to wait for his presents, didn't he?'

'Our baby Jesus is a doll. Will you come and see me be an angel? Daddy's made me a halo to wear.'

Mike caught his breath, waiting for Grace's answer. He thought she looked touched and very pleased to be asked.

'I'd love to,' she said. 'When is it?'

He cleared his throat. 'Tuesday afternoon in the church, with a repeat performance on Sunday. You have no idea what strict instructions we've been given about when to get there and which carols to practise and to make sure they all know their lines and don't wear coloured knickers under the angel dresses. This isn't a nativity—it's show business!'

Grace laughed. When had that rich tone started making him tingle? 'It will be lovely,' she said, getting into the car. 'My friend Liz is a bit of a perfectionist, that's all, and the Reverend Christine wants her first Christmas here to really stand out.'

'Believe me, it will! I'm willing to sing "Once in Royal David's City" just one more time but then that's it till next Christmas.'

'I'd better go, Mike. Try not to fall down any more on your way to the manor.'

'I'll do my best.' He shut the door for her, waited for her to wind down the window to say goodbye. 'Oh, did you see I found the gates? Eventually I'll have an electric system fitted so you can open them without getting out of the car.'

'That would have shocked the people who originally built the house.'

'Cheaper than employing a full-time gate-keeper.' He studied her face. 'What's the matter?'

She shook her head as if impatient with herself and started the car. 'Nothing. The gates are great. I suppose I'm just taking longer than I expected to get used to the change.'

'But you liked the thought of the secret passage being unblocked. You liked the idea of the kitchen being thrown open and a conservatory added.'

She raised her voice to carry over the sound of the engine. 'Yes, I did. Don't worry about it, Mike. I'm being irrational. Bye, Bethany.'

He and Bethany watched her drive off up the village street, then they resumed their walk to the manor. What was wrong with the gates? They were safe, practical, original… She *was* being irrational. All the same, her words about it taking time to get used to change started an interesting train of thought in his mind.

The cold weather was starting to take its toll. Grace had a lot more calls than normal from patients who wondered whether she could just call in on her way past rather than them travel into Rivercut. She was finishing typing up her notes for the day when there was a tap on her door. Mike on his way to start his evening surgery.

'Grace, I was wondering about instigating a weekly review of the patients that don't pass through my or Dad's hands. Just to keep us aware of any problems that might be brewing.'

Grace looked at him levelly. There was a touch

too much innocent helpfulness in his tone. 'This wouldn't be about you deciding whether I should or shouldn't go out on my own time to patients, would it? Because a district nurse is generally held to be autonomous and capable of making up her own mind as to whether she's needed or not.'

'Nurse Fellowes, I wouldn't dream of calling your professional judgement into question!'

Grace raised her eyebrows. 'But?'

Mike sighed. 'But I've seen your workload. I'm not sure your heart knows the difference between genuinely needy and taking advantage.'

She was torn between irritation at the interference and warmth that he cared about her doing too much. 'Away to your patients, Dr Curtis. You're just going to have to trust me until we're less busy.'

All the same, because of the extra calls she was late finishing and late leaving, and more tired than normal when she got home. Maybe Mike had a point, she thought as she climbed the stairs wearily and fell into bed.

Next morning she realised with horror that she'd either slept through the alarm or had forgotten to set it. She washed hastily, dressed, grabbed the local paper out of the letterbox and hurried up to the surgery for her regular Tuesday clinic without stopping for breakfast. She got a couple of odd looks from people on the way, but it wasn't until she slipped into the surgery kitchen for a coffee in a short lull between patients and opened *The Moors News* that she found out why. There on the third page was the announcement of an engagement and an article—with photographs—about the engagement party at a posh country house hotel.

MATCH OF THE YEAR, it was headed. Prominent landowner Raymond Threlkeld had apparently had great pleasure in announcing the betrothal of his only daughter, Lorna, to local solicitor Peter Cox. He had welcomed many eminent county residents to an opulent dinner-dance in order to celebrate alongside the happy couple.

There followed a list of said guests, a description of the menu and a report on the male half of the happy couple's speech. 'I have spent my whole life looking for a woman like Lorna,' he said, looking deeply into his fiancée's eyes. 'And now I have found her.'

Grace felt sick. *I have spent my whole life looking for a woman like Lorna.* Those were words Peter had used to her as well. Just at this moment she didn't think she would ever trust a man again.

The door opened and Mike dashed in. 'Excellent, you've got the kettle on. I could kill for a mug of… Grace? What's up?'

'Nothing.' She fumbled a second mug out of the cupboard and put a spoonful of coffee into it. She heard the rustle of newspaper, an intake of breath.

'Oh, Grace.' Mike's arms came around her in a comforting hug. Just for a moment it was so nice to be held like that. He moved his lips to her ear. 'You really should have let me punch him, you know.'

Grace gave a shaky laugh. 'He'd sue you. Thanks, Mike. I'm all right.' She splashed milk quickly into her mug and headed back to her room. Any more of that and she'd melt. She *wanted* to melt. But that would be a disaster. She needed to be Nurse Fellowes again, professional and in control.

'I still say he was mad,' Mike called after her.

Several patients' heads swivelled interestedly. *Oh, thank you, Mike,* thought Grace.

'Getting on well with young Dr Curtis, are you?' wheezed her next patient.

'He's a very good doctor,' said Grace repressively. She slipped the blood-pressure cuff on and set the timer. 'Relax, please.'

But gossip was life blood to Mrs Smithson. 'We've all been saying how suitable it would be, what with his poor little girl motherless and you not getting any younger. And when we heard how your car was outside the surgery all night last week, well, we were pleased as punch. Nobody's worried about that sort of thing these days, are they?'

'I had a meal with both the doctors Curtis and there was wine, which is why I walked home. Your blood pressure's fine, Mrs Smithson. Now, can you breathe deeply and then blow as hard as possible into this tube for me? See how efficiently your lungs are working.'

Not as efficiently as the local grapevine, that was for sure. Grace went through the rest of the checks resolving to be discreet with a capital D in her future dealings with the Curtis household.

The Nativity play was to be at two o'clock in the church. Grace had a couple of visits to make in the village, but got a phone call while she was at Mrs Johnson's house to ask if she could pop in to see Mr Harris, whose daughter was concerned that he'd had a dizzy spell. Unfortunately, Mr Harris lived at the other end of Rivercut, which meant by the time Grace had got there, diagnosed the problem and hurried to St Lawrence's she was late. Not to worry, she'd slip into the back and would still be able to tell Bethany truthfully that she'd watched the whole thing.

First problem—there was standing room only. Evidently the school parents wanted to make a good impression on the new vicar. Also, a good half of them had camcorders. She'd be continually in the way. Second problem—Mike was twisting round from his position in the front pew, looking for her. When he saw her he beckoned that he'd saved her a place. Oh, great. Grace walked the entire length of the aisle feeling as if her face was blazing as brightly as Rudolph's nose.

'All okay?' he asked in a low voice. 'Do I need to see Mr Harris?'

'Not unless you take a glass with you,' Grace murmured back. 'He'd smuggled himself in a bottle of whisky and had started on the

Christmas cheer early. I'm not surprised he'd had a dizzy spell.'

Mike chuckled. 'I'm glad you're here,' he said simply.

How could he make her heart ache with just one sentence? 'Is everything all right backstage?' she asked. 'Not too much stage fright?'

'Couple of nasty moments when the halos slipped on the walk up here from school, but otherwise they seem to be all right.'

The organ started playing. Good, she didn't have to talk any more.

Christine—Rivercut's new vicar—welcomed the audience and said how happy she was that the youngest children at the school had chosen a traditional Nativity to perform on this, her first Christmas here. Then there was a scuffle in the screened-off side chapel and Liz was heard exhorting the shepherds to get out into the nave and start watching their flocks. The play had begun.

The moment the angels filed in, Mike grasped Grace's hand. She couldn't blame him. Bethany looked enchanting. Perhaps she spoiled it a bit by looking into the audience and smiling widely at Grace and Mike, but most of the children did that. It added to the charm.

Strangely, though, it was when Mary and Joseph came on stage, looking for an inn to stay the night, that Grace broke down. Tears ran down her face. Over twenty years ago she had played the pregnant Mary and she had loved it. And now a child that she…that she loved was taking part in the same play.

Mike saw her tears and squeezed her fingers before passing her a tissue. After she'd dried her eyes he didn't take her hand again. She told herself this was sensible. There was enough talk as it was.

It was a magical afternoon. Everyone remembered their lines or were gently prompted by Liz. Bethany was a wonderful angel and spoke clearly. The familiar carols sung in children's voices brought a lump to her throat. The Christmas story ended, the cast lined up, smiling and waving in relief; the applause was tumultuous.

'I need to collect Bethany,' said Mike over the noise.

Grace nodded. She'd wait for them outside. It was too busy in here and she wanted to be alone to collect her thoughts for a moment. She threaded her way through the press of parents to the church door, twisted the iron ring and stepped out into a world where the sun was just disappearing behind a bank of lowering snow-laden clouds.

Straight into the path of Peter Cox and Lorna Threlkeld.

'Well, well,' said Peter. 'Fancy seeing you here.'

Grace stiffened. 'If you wanted the Nativity, you've just missed it.'

'Why would we?' drawled Lorna. 'I get enough of kids at the stables. We're here to see the vicar about arranging our wedding.'

'Come to that, why are you here, Grace? You don't have any—' Peter broke off, looking into the church. 'Oh, I see. Congratulations. You really have found someone to keep you and the manor in the style to which you'd like to be accustomed, haven't you? Quick work.'

Grace turned to see Mike hoisting Bethany in his arms, about to set off up the aisle.

Peter was still talking, softly poisonous. 'And a surrogate child too to slake those maternal longings. Clever Grace. You get his gratitude and an instant family in one fell swoop.'

Mike had been detained, talking to the mother

of one of Bethany's friends. Thank goodness for small mercies. 'You're wrong,' said Grace between set teeth. 'There is nothing between Dr Curtis and myself except work.'

'Don't give me that. A widower with the inconvenience of a small child? You're a gift from the gods, Grace. Over-sexed, pathetically grateful and poor. And right on his doorstep.'

Lorna laughed and linked her arm in Peter's. 'A match made in Heaven, in fact. Come on, darling. The vicar must be finished with this lot by now, surely?'

They strolled inside. The parents and children streaming out blocked Grace's view of the nave. She felt ill. Sick and shaken. Was it true? What Peter had said? Was she all those horrible things? And was Mike taking advantage of her?

Her phone went. One of her more cantankerous patients wanted to know how much longer she was going to be. Grace had never been more pleased in her life to hurry off.

Away from the church.

Away from people.

Away from Mike.

CHAPTER ELEVEN

MIKE zipped Bethany into her coat, picked up the bag with her school clothes in and hoisted her into his arms. It was going to be easier getting out of the church if he was carrying her rather than worrying about her tripping everyone up. Bethany was pouring an excited monologue into his ear, but for once he wasn't giving her his full attention. Where was Grace? He'd assumed she'd be waiting for them. He couldn't believe she wasn't by the door. He'd felt so close to her, watching the Nativity. It had almost been like… Almost been as if they were a family. He looked down the street through the thinning crowd of parents—and saw her Land Rover pull away from the side of the road. Of course. He'd forgotten she'd be still working this afternoon. She must be on her way to her next appointment. He set Bethany on her feet—an angel in anorak and

Wellington boots—and trudged back home with her, feeling flat with disappointment.

There was no message from Grace on the surgery phone or his mobile. Once evening surgery was over and Bethany in James's care, Mike walked down to the cottage.

'Hi,' he said, when she opened the door. 'I wondered if you fancied a drink at the pub?'

'Last time we had a drink at the pub we ended up in bed.' She looked normal, she sounded normal, but she wasn't quite. If she'd been a patient, Mike would have said she was hiding something. 'And that was bad?' he asked, probing lightly.

'No, it was very good indeed, as well you know. But I don't want to be a habit, Mike. I don't want to be a convenience.'

'You weren't!' he said, stung by the injustice. 'Can I come inside? I think we need to talk about this.'

Grace moved to let him in. 'You haven't mentioned that evening,' she muttered.

'Neither have you.' He sat down on the sofa. 'If you must know, when I got back Bethany was—'

Grace's phone shrilled, interrupting him. She

answered it. 'Hi, Robert! No, I haven't forgotten your offer… Yes, well, you know Natalie. I just hope her credit card's made of stern stuff.' She listened a moment more. 'I'll let you know. Have a good Christmas. Thanks for ringing.'

'An offer?' said Mike, before he could stop himself. What was the matter with him? Why did he feel so aggressive all of a sudden?

After a moment's hesitation she perched next to him. 'Robert Ross is an old friend from my training days. He's setting up a back-to-basics teaching department for hands-on nurses. He was trying to convince me I should move to Manchester.'

Alarm, rage, *something* swept over Mike. 'You can't. You're needed here. You belong here!'

She blinked. 'I'm only the district nurse. I'm easily replaceable.'

'Any other district nurse might be—not you. You're special. Who else is going to turn out to patients at unsocial hours because they can't work the childproof cap on their tablets?' He was trying desperately to hold on to his sense of humour, but he was filled with such horror at the thought of her leaving Rivercut that he was having difficulty stringing a sentence together.

She was looking at him oddly again. 'Relax, I'm not going. Or I don't think I am.'

Oh, thank goodness. He reached for her in relief, drew her towards him. Their lips met in a clash of urgency and need.

A brief, sweet moment and then she drew back. 'Mike, I can't do this tonight. I don't know what I want, and I don't think you know what you want, either.'

He wanted *her*, that's what he wanted. But dimly, through his frustration, he recognised that telling her so would probably be counter-productive.

She was talking again. 'Can you give me a few days? I'm sorry, Mike, but I really need to think something through.'

What could he say? No matter that all he felt like doing right now was dragging her to the nearest cave and barricading the pair of them inside.

'Sure,' he said, getting up. 'I'll go and have that pint.' At least the temperature outside was as good as a cold shower.

By Thursday afternoon, Grace was feeling thoroughly frustrated. Mike had taken her at her word and not raised the subject of their relationship again. He appeared to be settling into the district well and was finding his way about. A bit too well, actually. Grace dropped in at Holroyd Farm to see Edith and was surprised to see his Range Rover coming the other way out of the farmyard. Just checking on those new tablets, she was told when she asked. Grace was niggled—Mrs Holroyd was supposed to be *her* patient.

Still, it was now Bethany's last riding lesson before Christmas and Grace had picked her up from school and was helping her change. She happened to know that Mike had bought his daughter a complete riding outfit for Christmas—Grace wished she could see the little girl's face when she opened the present on Christmas Day. In fact, she wished…

No. She must stop thinking that way. Mike was still in love with his dead wife. She and Mike might be attracted to each other, but a relationship based on physical needs and her own neediness would be doomed to disaster.

At the previous lesson, Bethany had graduated to going around the ring without needing to be led, so Grace leant on the rail and watched her. It was so sweet, all the ponies had tinsel twined into their tack and the children had been promised the treat of feeding their mounts a Christmas carrot each at the end of the lesson. It reminded her of years ago when she too had started learning to ride.

A low, furious voice broke in on Grace's thoughts. 'Why the hell aren't you in the ring with her?'

Grace jumped, startled. 'Mike, she told you last week when we got home that she could ride by herself.'

'I didn't realise she meant all the time! She's far too small and inexperienced. What if the horse bolts?'

'She's coming on really well and these ponies are so old and staid they wouldn't know how to bolt. Calm down.'

'Easy for you to say, she's not your… Oh, no, that's too fast…'

The circle of children had increased to a trot. Grace smiled at the look of delight on Bethany's face. The little girl saw Mike and beamed, then blinked and slid off the pony's side. Mike instantly made to vault over the rail, but Grace hung on to him. The circle had slowed and one of the riding instructors was already there, picking Bethany up.

'Oh, well done! You fell beautifully. Just as we told you, no feet tangled in stirrups, no hanging on to the reins, nothing. What a clever girl you are. Up we get again.'

Mike was incandescent, trying to pull away from Grace's restraining grip. 'That does it, she's never riding again ever.'

'She's already back on the pony. Does she seem worried?'

'She's too young to know the danger!'

'Mike, you can't keep her wrapped in cotton wool for ever.'

'I lost her mother. I'm not going to lose her as well. Let me go!'

'No. You're going to stay here and watch and smile and be proud. If you leave, she's going to think you were disappointed when she fell off. If you take her away, she's going to think she's done something bad and be upset.'

He looked at her, his eyes blazing. 'You don't know what you're asking me.'

Inside, Grace cried. Outside, she remained calm. 'I do! This is important, Mike. Your dad is always saying how like you Bethany is in temperament. "Never walked when he could run," remember? You *have* to let Bethany push her own boundaries. How else is she going to grow? Did James ever stop you climbing trees, even though you might fall out of them? Did he forbid you to jump in the deep end of the swimming pool? Riding is only dangerous if you haven't been taught properly. Bethany is being taught properly.'

Mike didn't say a word, just shook her off and stared ahead at the ring in silence, his whole body rigid. After five minutes, he rasped, 'Have I watched for long enough now? May I go?' He waved to his daughter, turned and left.

After the lesson was over, the carrots duly given to the ponies and Christmas wishes exchanged all round, Grace strapped Bethany into her car. No Lorna this week—that was good. She was still shaking with reaction after the exchange with Mike; any more unkind words would probably finish her off. She *hated* telling people home truths, but at least doing it in the line of work meant she had proven medical research to back it up. Why should Mike believe her about Bethany? Especially after the trauma he'd been through. He had every right to hate her for telling him to loosen up with his daughter.

Drearily, Grace drove back. She automatically glanced up the drive of the manor as they passed. Mike's car was there. Her heart twisted.

'There's Daddy!' squealed Bethany.

Grace took a deep breath and turned in between the new-old gates. Her headlights illuminated a solitary figure swinging an axe at a log pile.

'Daddy,' said Bethany excitedly as soon as he opened her door. 'I gived Foxtrot a carrot!'

'That's lovely, darling.'

He looked so, so tired. Grace ached for him. She cleared her throat. 'Is the kitchen still working?' she asked. 'I could kill for a cup of tea.'

Her voice sounded strange. Hopefully Mike would accept the olive branch.

It was touch and go for a moment, then, 'I think we could run to that.' He unfastened Bethany and lifted her out. 'Foxtrot's the horse that's ten feet tall with a mouth full of teeth, I take it?'

Grace's heart banged painfully. 'Oh, more like twenty feet tall. With a dreadful temper and a trigger-happy kick.'

Mike gave a lopsided smile. 'Grace, I'm sorry. I overreacted.'

She laid a hand on his arm. 'You had reason. Goodness, haven't you made the hall look bright?'

'Scrubs up nicely, doesn't it?'

It did. The panelling had been cleaned, the floor polished and the ceiling whitewashed. She only now appreciated how careworn it had got.

'Come and see my bedroom,' shouted Bethany, tugging her towards the stairs.

Oh, no. No, Grace wasn't at all ready for that. Another little girl in her room. Someone else's decor in the sanctuary she had known all her life. Different curtains framing 'her' view of the moors.

'Go on,' murmured Mike. 'Be brave.'

She supposed she deserved that. She girded up her courage and followed Bethany. And was astonished beyond measure when the little girl danced along the passageway to what had been Grace's parents' room.

'It had the princess bed in,' explained Mike. 'Would your mother have approved?'

Grace looked dazedly around the freshly decorated corner room. The bed canopy was now pale pink. The wallpaper had unicorns, fairies, rainbows, hearts and butterflies on a pink back-ground. 'Definitely,' she said. 'A fairy bower. Mum didn't live in the real world either.'

She was shown the rest of the rooms on the way back down to the kitchen. The nursery she had designed with so much love was untouched. She didn't know whether to be pleased or unset-tled. The other rooms looked much as she re-membered them, though there was something different, something she couldn't quite put her finger on. It wasn't until she had finished her mug of tea and was preparing to leave that she realised what it was.

'Mike! The upstairs rooms! The paintwork… the papering… They look exactly the same as when I left, only brand-new! Why would you re-create the house as it was?'

He looked just a tiny bit disconcerted. 'I suppose I liked the way it was,' he said evasively. 'It was easier to restore it rather than dream up something new. The architect I asked to check the building out was enthralled. He said he'd never seen a small manor house like this one with so much apparently original work. He's got some excellent suggestions for how to modernise the plumbing and heating without it being intrusive.'

'I see. It's going to be lovely.'

'I hope so.' He glanced at her. 'So do you think you can bear to come to the party?'

Grace frowned. What party?

'Bethany! Didn't you give Grace the invitation?'

'Oops.' Bethany giggled. 'I forgot. Sorry.' She raced down the remaining stairs, peered into her school backpack and pulled out a rather crumpled envelope. 'Here you are! I helped Daddy write it and I signed it and he says it's my party as well as his and I can have a new dress that's long just like you.' She thrust the envelope into Grace's hand and added, 'I drawed the holly. It's good, isn't it?'

'Very good.' Grace opened the letter—an invitation from Miss Bethany Curtis and Dr Michael Curtis to a celebratory party at the manor on Christmas Eve. She swallowed. There had always been a Christmas Eve party at the manor. But her family had organised it. It would be different going as a guest.

'You can come?' Bethany pleaded.

'Of course I can come. Nothing would keep me away. I shall write you a proper reply this evening.'

'You've got to. That's what RSVP means. It's so Daddy doesn't buy too many packets of crisps.'

'And you're going to have a long dress. That's exciting.'

'She's been looking at your old photographs,' said Mike. 'I'll ask one of Sarah's friends to send something up. They've been bombarding me with emails for a fortnight, wanting to know what to send us from civilisation.'

Grace lowered her voice and leant towards his ear. 'If it's any help, I bought one for her in Manchester as a Christmas present.'

It was lovely, being this close to him. But all he said was, 'Grace, that's fantastic. Do you want to give it her before Christmas Day? She'll be over the moon.'

After Bethany was in bed, Mike sat with his father, watching television.

'You all right, lad?' asked James.

Mike sighed. 'Just thinking.'

James cleared his throat. 'I know we haven't been close these past few years, and neither of us are good at saying what we feel—but I do want you to be happy. I got the feeling that you and Grace might…'

'Dad, it's complicated.'

There was a small silence. James sipped his whisky. 'Sarah wouldn't have wanted you to mourn for ever.'

But when was the right time to stop? Grace was lovely—her dark blonde hair, her wide smile, the way she wanted to eradicate all suffering everywhere. The truth was that Mike wanted to be with her all the time. He'd refreshed the manor because of her distress at the changes. He couldn't care less what it looked like as long as she was happy. Her honesty this afternoon at the stables had been devastating—but she'd been right, reluctant though he was to admit it.

But how could he betray Sarah's memory by even contemplating sharing his and Bethany's lives with another woman? Was he quite sure it wasn't just his bodily needs that were driving him? At the thought of Grace's body an exquisite cramp gripped him. He wondered what his father would say if he went down there now, tonight. Come to that, he wondered what Grace would say. He needed to know her better. He would ask her to have lunch with them again tomorrow. He would talk to her—really talk. Show her he'd heeded her advice. Find out about *her*, her hopes and dreams and aspirations. And, meanwhile, he would carry on with his plans for the party.

The next day, however, fate seemed determined to thwart him. It had snowed again overnight and when Mike put his head around Grace's door he found no one there. So many patients had cancelled that Grace was doing house visits instead, the receptionist told him cheerfully. He rang her mobile at once.

'Hi, Mike.'

'Grace, what do you think you are doing?'

She chuckled. 'My rounds.'

It was unfair of him to feel cross at a perfectly good answer, but he'd wanted to see her—how much he hadn't realised until this minute—and a crackly phone call was no substitute. 'Did it not occur to you that if the weather conditions are too bad for your patients to come to you, they are also too bad for you to go to them?'

'My patients are old and frail, so it's not the

same thing at all. And the roads aren't too bad—don't forget that we are used to the snow up here, not like you Londoners.'

That hurt. 'So used to it that you needed me to pull you out of that ditch the first time we met!'

'Now you're being petty. And I need to concentrate and my battery's low. Bye, Mike.'

He exhaled irritably and called for his first patient. An hour later he decided maybe he *had* been petty. He tried to ring Grace again but got voicemail. *Please leave your message after the tone.* Mike was flummoxed. What did he want to say? 'I, er… Just drive carefully. No heroics. Don't go and see anyone who doesn't need it. Call me when you get back.'

He returned to his own list, even more disgruntled. There was nothing from her by the time he had to collect Bethany. Everyone at Rivercut Primary was hugely excited by it being the end of term. They raced around the playground, scraping together snowballs and skidding in the slush. Their parents stamped feet to keep warm, balancing bags of this term's artwork and exchanging last-minute Christmas cards. Mike smiled and wished people all the joy of the season, but his mind was on an elderly Land Rover somewhere up in the tops of the hills. He held Bethany's hand tightly.

The sky was leaden and grey now. Thick flakes of snow fell on them on the way home, that morning's footprints filling fast. Grace's cottage was lifeless, her car nowhere to be seen.

Mike knew it was probably just because he wasn't used to conditions on the North Yorkshire moors, but he was really uneasy. He checked his phone—nothing. He called Grace and got voice-mail again. James hadn't heard anything either but, then—as he pointed out—he wouldn't have expected to. 'District nurses are autonomous. They don't have to account to us for all their comings and goings.'

'Well, that's going to change for a start,' said Mike grumpily. He left James and Bethany making pancakes—an exercise they both enjoyed—and opened the connecting door to the surgery for a last prowl around.

There was a note on his desk. Grace must have rung while he'd been at school. She was all right. Thank goodness. Then he frowned. The recep-tionist had written that the road from Kender

Downfall was blocked so Grace would put up at the pub on the main road for the night.

Mike stared at it. Where on earth was Kender Downfall? Which pub would it be? So many things he didn't know! His eyes fell on his computer. Grimly he switched it on and pulled up Grace's diary, laboriously tracking her route around the high moors. A couple of questions to James and he had the name of the pub. He phoned it—ready to blast her for her stupidity in going out to such inhospitable places in appalling weather.

A few moments later he was back in the kitchen doorway.

'Found her?' said James, pouring batter into the frying pan. Then he turned and looked at Mike's face. 'What's up?'

'The pub is full of people but she's not one of them.' His heart was thudding against his chest. 'Can you look after Bethany? All night if need be?'

'Of course, but shouldn't you leave it to the rescue people? Dusk's falling. You don't know your way about these hills yet.'

Mike gave a strained smile. 'No, but my sat nav thinks it does. Time to see if it can put its money where its mouth is.'

'Be careful, lad.'

'I will.' He dropped a kiss on Bethany's head. 'I've got too much to live for.'

Where the hell was she?

CHAPTER TWELVE

IT WAS going to be a whiter-than-white
Christmas, thought Grace as she drove carefully
along the snow-packed roads, blessing her new
tyres. It was nice that Mike had phoned that
morning, nice that he was concerned enough to
forgive her interference yesterday, but right now
the deserted landscape, the relentless wind and
the whirling snow suited her mood. In her trusty
vehicle she was the sheriff of the moors, with a
hypodermic on each hip instead of a six-shooter.
She brought comfort and reassurance. She kept
the dreaded spectre of hospital in-patient wards
at bay. She made it possible for her people to live
the independent lives they wanted. And if the
thought strayed across her mind that it would be
nice to come home from all this to a warm house
with a loving partner and a scamp of a little girl
to cuddle, Grace ignored it. Mike needed to sort

out his own life—she wasn't going to get in the way of that again.

She glanced at her watch—it was touch and go, but she thought she had time to squeeze in one last call. Nellie Farthing had mentioned that her foot was a bit sore, if Grace happened to be passing this way. Grace had decided to be 'passing' as soon as possible. Nellie was eighty-three and too tough for her own good. She lived with family who would soon ring if there was an urgent problem, but Grace wasn't convinced Nellie always told them the 'silly little things' that bothered her.

Because of the driving conditions it took longer than usual to get to Longsky farm. The place was well named. It stood on a hilltop, the highest point for miles. The views on a good day were entrancing. Today—with a sinking heart—all Grace could see were advancing stormclouds.

Still, she was welcomed, told she was mad to come out in weather like this, given a mug of tea. Then she took the ever-cheerful Nellie into her bedroom for a quick examination. She was glad she had done so. Some time ago Nellie had had herpes zoster—shingles—and it had been painful. The pain had not quite disappeared. This was a condition known as post-herpetic neural-gia. Grace decided to give her more analgesics.

There was another problem with the sole of Nellie's left foot. She had developed an ulcer that would not heal—largely because she kept walking on it. Grace scolded, cleaned and dressed it, and obtained a promise that Nellie would spend less time standing and more time with her feet up. 'I'll be back in a week or so, but if your foot gets bad again, phone at once. I'm going to tell your son and daughter-in-law.'

'I feel much better already,' said Nellie. Grace thought that if this was true it would be a medical miracle—but she didn't say anything.

Nellie's son was waiting for her at the front door. 'Weather's taken a turn for the worse,' he said. 'Look at that snow fly. And it's falling dark too. I reckon you ought to stay the night.'

She shook her head. 'No need. Once I'm behind Kender Downfall I'll be in a bit of a shadow. The wind and snow will be less there.'

'Well, come back if there's any trouble. Or phone me and I'll come and fetch you on the tractor.'

'I will, that's a promise. Merry Christmas!' She ran to her Land Rover.

The weather was bad. Her windscreen wipers could only just keep the screen clear. The wind buffeted the car so it rocked, shaking her. The tyres had to fight for grip. A small voice in her head whispered that Mike might well have been right about her not going out on rounds today. Or at least cutting them short early. But she cheered herself by reflecting that Nellie at least had needed her. That ulcer on her foot could have got really nasty if left any longer. She drove on carefully, slowly, knowing that she would get home eventually.

Coming down the steep slope into Kender Downfall was more like sledging than driving. But she made it, and progressed along the narrow road around the hill on the far side. And there with a jerk, she stopped—an inch from deep, piled snow. No way was she getting any further. There had been a mini-avalanche, the road was covered with loose snow to a depth of several feet. She sighed. This was what came of being awkward.

She considered her options. She shared the general country view of people who got into trouble through their own stupidity, blithely expecting others to sort them out. The first thing she must do was reassure anyone who might worry about her, but she certainly wasn't going to ring Mike and tell him he'd been right! With the last of her phone battery she called surgery Reception instead, saying she wouldn't be back that night because of the bad weather. She would stay at the pub on the main road. Would the receptionist tell anyone who asked?

It was a likely enough story—the Drovers' Rest a few miles away was constantly putting up marooned travellers—but Grace had no intention of going there. She had a full 'stranded' kit in her car—a sleeping bag, blankets, a complete set of winter clothing and Kendal mint cake. From time to time she could start the engine to warm the inside of the car. The thing to do was not to panic. In a way she was half enjoying herself.

She kept the car engine running while she swiftly stripped off her nurse's uniform and pulled on heavy walking gear. Most important, a woolly hat pulled right down over her ears. A quarter of the body's heat could be lost through the head and neck. Then she reclined the passenger seat, wriggled into the sleeping bag (not as easy as survival handbooks made it look), wrapped blankets round herself for good measure, and lay down to sleep. She was just a bit disturbed by the snow piling up on the windscreen and tried the radio to see if there were any weather alerts. Sadly, the signal was so badly distorted as to be unrecognisable. And it was a nuisance getting her arm in and out of the sleeping bag.

Grace dozed, and woke again with Mike's image in her mind. Now, what was the point of that? But her subconscious didn't know any better. To make sure it got the message, she said 'I love Mike Curtis' out loud. Then added the killer sentence. 'But he doesn't love me.' The words formed a tiny cloud of condensation over her lips.

Does it matter?

Now, that was a revolutionary thought. Mike was attracted to her physically. He cared for her in a friendly way, felt responsible for her. Did it matter that he didn't love her to the exclusion of all else?

She dozed again, worrying away at the problem she'd set herself. Then she woke and frowned. The windscreen was solid with snow, but there was a small light bobbing up and down on the road outside. She struggled to get her arm free and wound down her side window, shivering at the blast of cold air and snow.

A light was coming towards her. A small light and a darker shadow behind it. A light carried by a man. The light flashed onto her face. A moment later the shadow stopped beside the car. 'What the hell do you think you're doing?' it said forcefully.

Mike Curtis's voice. Grace blinked, unable to take it in. Was she having hallucinations? Could one hallucinate a voice? 'Um, sleeping,' she said.

'Is the driver's door unlocked?'

'Yes. I didn't expect many thieves down here tonight. And I took the ignition key out.'

'Do you know there are times when you have too much to say?'

He disappeared round to the other side of the car. She shut her window, adjusted the seat so that it was upright again. From outside she heard the sounds of a man brushing the snow from his clothes. Then the door was opened, a rucksack bundled in—landing heavily on her lap—and Mike followed.

He sat in the driver's seat, grunting as he adjusted it to make space for his legs. From out of the rucksack he took a Thermos, poured a drink and handed it to her. 'Here. Drink this before we start arguing.'

The smell of coffee filled the car. She thought just that would be enough to revive her, but the coffee itself was even more blissful. She had to say something. 'Do you know, I could kiss you for this?'

'I don't make a practice of kissing people I'm about to have a flaming row with.'

'It's all right, it was just a figure of speech. Mike, why have you come out here when I sent a message saying that I was all right?'

'Because I want to shout at you very loudly and you aren't answering your damn phone! How stupid can you get, Grace? I found your message on my desk! I might not have known at all. You hadn't even had the courage to ring me yourself. "The pub on the main road" indeed— anything less helpful would be hard to imagine. I worked out where you'd been and phoned everywhere along the route. Longsky farm said you'd left in dreadful weather, even though you'd been offered a bed for the night! Dad told me about the Drovers' Rest, so I phoned them, intending to give you hell—and you weren't there! So I guessed you were stuck. I put my faith in the sat nav and arrived on the other side of this snow-dump.'

Grace finished her coffee, feeling better by the minute. 'Only to find that I was well wrapped up and sleeping peacefully.'

'You were shivering.'

'Because you opened the door! I would have been warm enough all night long otherwise.'

'I doubt that.'

She decided not to argue. 'Anyway, I do appreciate the coffee. And now I suppose you're going to frogmarch me back to your car and take me home. Shall I bring the Kendal mint cake?'

'You've got to be joking. Have you seen the weather out there? It's evil! I've used up all my luck getting here—I'm not driving anywhere else tonight.'

Grace looked at him blankly. 'Then what was the point coming to find me?'

'So I'd know you were safe! Look, I passed a barn a hundred yards or so back—that'll be safer and warmer than sleeping in the car, won't it?'

'I suppose so.' She paused a moment and reluctantly added, 'Thank you for coming to find me. It was good of you.'

'I suspect you'd have done the same for me—if only to prove what an idiot I was. Come on, let's go. What do you need to take from here?'

'Everything. Have you got a sleeping bag?'

'I've got the full kit. Following your example, remember?'

'Right,' she said gloomily. 'I'll put on my boots.' She wasn't exactly comfortable—but she was settled. Still, what he said made sense.

It was freezing outside the car, the wind cut through all her layers of clothes. Mike hoisted his rucksack onto his back, helped her into hers, took her arm and led her through the snow. His torch flickered. Without a word she got hers out of her pocket and flashed it on.

It seemed very hard work, pushing through the blizzard to the barn, but once inside the relief from the wind was immense. 'Sit there,' he said, and started hauling bales of hay to make a draught-proof wall.

'Not a chance,' she replied. She hung the torch on a convenient nail and did her share of dragging bales of hay together until they had constructed a small nest.

'Cosy for the night,' he said. 'By the way, I

never asked, you're not wet, are you? No falling into streams or anything?'

'I'm perfectly dry. Not even the snow has wetted me.'

'Good. I wouldn't want you to have to take your clothes off so I could warm you with the heat of my body.'

'I'd rather freeze, thank you.'

'Even if I bribed you with a sandwich and the rest of the coffee? Body heat is still something we have to conserve. I was going to suggest we zip our sleeping bags together and cuddle up to keep warm.'

Grace scrutinised his face. Was he joking? Half joking? 'Mike, we'll be wearing all our clothes.'

He looked unperturbed. 'Of course. It would be stupid to do otherwise. It means we won't notice the crumbs.'

She laughed. 'You're impossible. Let's do it. Boots off, though.'

There was a surprising amount of room in the zipped-together sleeping bags. They sat in them first of all, drinking the coffee and eating the sandwiches he had brought. Grace told him about Nellie Farthing, pointing out with only minor triumph that the old lady had indeed needed to see a nurse. It was odd—intimate in a strangely non-invasive way.

Mike got out to turn off the torch, and she held her breath as he slid back in beside her. 'Go to sleep,' he said, his voice deep and comforting. 'I'm not about to make advances.'

Pity, she thought, and matched his chaste kiss on the cheek with one of her own. But it was no good, she couldn't sleep. She loved him, and here he was lying next to her. And even if it had been unnecessary, he had come out in evil conditions to rescue her. It was bound to have an effect.

She was surprisingly warm, much warmer than she had been in the car. Various layers of clothes, sleeping bag and then hay, they all warmed her. And Mike's body heat, though he had rolled to the other edge of the sleeping bag.

'You know, it'll get colder,' she murmured. 'And to maximise our body heat we should be closer together.'

'You mean it might be sensible to hug each other to keep warm?'

'I think it could.'

Well, of course, it made sense. They wriggled

together. Grace found herself with one of Mike's arms under her neck, the other round her waist. Their bodies were pressed together, one of his thighs was over hers. She buried her face naturally into his neck and felt his lips against her hair.

'I've missed you so much, Grace,' he breathed.

He'd missed her? Grace pulled back in shock, straining to see his face in the irregular bars of moonlight. He'd missed *her*? Not Sarah? She made some sort of disbelieving, inarticulate sound.

And then he kissed her.

There was a world of longing in that kiss. And it felt so right, so very right. Had he come all this way, in this weather, to kiss her? And to do other things, judging by the way his hand had bypassed several layers of clothes in order to tug her vest out from the waistband of her trousers? There had been no need to bother, he could have…

This was a pain! If she hadn't known before why people got undressed before they went to bed, she certainly knew now. But with an excess of fumbling it was possible to loosen this and that, to unzip, to ease these down a bit…

To feel suddenly flooded with heat. To cry out with desire. To experience his banked-up passion.

Mike gave a low laugh. 'I never thought I'd ever make love to a woman with woollen socks on up to my knees, whilst wearing a bobble hat.'

'And I never thought I'd have a vest, T-shirt, shirt and sweater tucked under my chin and the bobble of his woolly hat tickling my nose.'

'Sexy, isn't it? We ought to write an extra chapter for one of those sex manuals. How to make love in a sleeping bag in freezing conditions whilst fully dressed.'

Grace chuckled. 'I'd love to see the diagrams. Oh, Mike… Oh, yes… No… Oh!'

Outside there was the howling of the wind, the banging of a loose plank, the weight of the ever-falling snow. But inside they had made their own little world and they were happy in it.

Afterwards they tenderly pulled together various bits of loosened clothing and hugged each other warm again. Grace snuggled into Mike's side. 'I feel warm and happy and content. But shouldn't we talk?'

'No,' he said drowsily. 'Not now. For now let's just be.'

So she slept. Tomorrow would come soon enough.

* * *

In the morning, bright sunshine shone through various cracks in the barn walls and there was the clanking of a tractor outside. Grace blinked her eyes open. Heavens above! What time was it? She kissed the forehead of a still-sleeping Mike, wriggled out of bed, pulled on boots, zipped her anorak hastily over the haphazardness of her loosened clothes and went to look at the day.

The storm had blown itself out. It was noticeably warmer. Mike's car was parked outside the barn and Tom Farthing had just broken through the snowfall on his tractor.

'Want to move your car down next to the doctor's, Grace?' he called. 'Then I can clear the road properly.'

'Um, yes. Yes, of course.' She hurried to the Land Rover, fumbling for her keys. Was she blushing?

'That's grand,' shouted Tom over the noise of his engine, and chugged on his way.

Grace returned to the barn. Mike was sitting up in the sleeping bag, rooting around in his rucksack. 'Aha!' he said, and drew out a second flask. He waved it at her. 'Breakfast,' he said.

'Is that more coffee? Mike, you're a marvel!'

'Now and again. Was that the rescue brigade outside?'

'Only Tom Farthing, clearing the road. But I think our cover is blown.'

'Ah, well.'

He didn't say any more and Grace didn't push it, just drank her coffee, more lukewarm than hot. He'd talk when he was ready.

He slid out of the sleeping bag and they tidied up in a nearly companionable silence. 'It's very Swallows and Amazons, all this,' he remarked. 'I used to love the books when I was a boy. Sailing and camping and surviving in tough conditions.'

She laughed. 'And everyone living happily ever after.'

'Yes,' he said, his face sobering. 'That's the rub, isn't it? Children's stories always have happy endings. The burglars get caught, the horses escape the fire, the kids survive. Life isn't always like that.'

'No, it isn't,' she said. 'But sometimes enough good things happen that you can pretend it is.'

Had she said enough? She desperately hoped that he was going to open up to her. Surely after last night he'd have to admit they had the ability to make each other happy? It would do as a beginning.

But instead he hoisted his rucksack and took it out to his car. 'Grace, isn't it lovely here?'

The two of them looked around in silence. It was truly beautiful, the curves of the hills outlined by the sparkling white of the snow.

'Yes, it is lovely,' she agreed. 'I don't think I'll ever forget it.'

Another pause, the chance for him to say something more. 'Do you want to follow me back?' he said.

'Mike!'

He sighed. 'I know, Grace, I know. Listen— yesterday, for the first time in over a year, I didn't think about Sarah all day. I was too wound up thinking about you instead.'

And now she wished she hadn't provoked him. 'I'm sorry,' she said. Her stomach was solid with misery. 'I didn't mean to make you feel guilty.'

'You ridiculous woman! I'm not feeling guilty towards Sarah! I'm feeling guilty towards you for not being able to sort my emotions out!'

Was that good? She thought it might be. The misery melted a little. Now, should she tell him she loved him? Would that make his dilemma better? Or worse? 'Mike, I—'

He put his finger on her lips. 'Dear Grace, give me a day or two to wrestle. Right now I want to get home and have a hot shower.'

Ruefully, Grace had to admit that was what she wanted too. 'Snap. Would you and Bethany and James like to come to lunch tomorrow? Then Bethany can have her Christmas present in time for your party.'

'That would be lovely.'

With a sigh of relief, Grace stripped off the clothes she had worn all night and ran a bath. As she luxuriated in her favourite bath foam she thought about her lovemaking with Mike. It *had* been lovemaking. It had been fumbling, uncomfortable, awkward, at times almost impossible. But they had enjoyed it, the joy largely coming from the pleasure each was giving the other. There had been no mistaking that. At that moment Mike had really loved her. She just had to wait for him to realise it.

She hadn't intended inviting them for lunch, but it was a perfect way to establish friendly—

maybe more than friendly—relations. Except…
Oh, Lord, did they do traditional Sunday lunch?
And she only had a tiny freezer compartment,
there certainly wasn't a joint for four in it. She
hastily finished her bath and dashed up to the
butcher to see what he had left.

They were prompt the next day—which was
good, because Grace had started far too early.
Her kitchen wasn't big enough to spread the
preparations around. It had to be done task by
task. The living room wasn't big enough either,
even without the tree taking up so much room.
Grace banished the large cushion and unfolded
one wing of the table so they could all sit
together. Bethany thought it highly amusing that
she had to scramble over the arm of the couch to
get to her chair.

'We brought wine,' announced James, kissing
her on the cheek. 'Point me at the glasses and
I'll pour.'

Grace thought Mike was going to peck her on
the cheek as well, but at the last moment his lips
met hers, light but definite. Did that mean he'd
come to a decision? Or was it simply an ac-
knowledgement of something between them?

'If you don't like roast beef,' she said, bringing the joint to the table, 'I'd rather no one tells me. I would have done chicken, but with Christmas next week…'

'Quite right,' said Mike. 'This looks lovely. And all of us eat any amount of Yorkshire pudding. I'm afraid we even have it with turkey.'

So that was all right. And with a glass of wine inside her and everyone making trencherman-like inroads on the food, Grace felt herself relax.

'Where are you spending Christmas Day?' asked Mike at one point.

The question was casual, but Grace didn't miss his swift exchange of looks with his father. 'At Natalie's,' she said.

'That's nice. And I suppose you'll be working flat out until then, will you?' Mike sounded resigned rather than reproachful.

'People don't stop being ill just because it's the holiday season. You're not telling me the pair of you won't be on call?'

'Guilty,' said James cheerfully. 'And in that case, you'd better have my present to you early. It's an in-car charger for your phone. Can't have my district nurse going awol again.'

It seemed to be the cue for them to pile the washing up into the kitchen and move across to the tree. Bethany was ecstatic about her party dress, insisting on putting it on there and then.

'Beautiful,' said Mike. His eyes met Grace's. 'Thank you.' James was just as pleased with his bottle of whisky, but it was Mike's reaction that Grace really wanted to see. She handed over the carefully wrapped package, praying that he'd like it.

He did. He looked at the old map of Rivercut in its frame and his face lit up with joy. 'Grace, this is wonderful, it couldn't be more… You must have known…' He kissed her impetuously, unguardedly. 'It's just perfect.' And then he hesitated. 'My present to you isn't wrapped yet. I thought I'd give it to you when you come to the manor for the party on Christmas Eve.'

Grace felt just a tiny bit let down. It was a tactful way of saying he hadn't got her anything yet. 'That's fine,' she said. 'Who's for coffee?'

She kept herself busy over the next couple of days. Mike was looking after Bethany as there was no school, so he wasn't in the surgery. He wasn't idle, though. She seemed to be forever passing his Range Rover on the road. It was almost as if he'd committed her schedule to memory and was avoiding her. She couldn't work him out. Since that night in the barn she thought they'd come to some kind of understanding…but what? Ah, well, there was just his party to get through, then she'd be off to Natalie's where they could discuss the strangeness of men to their heart's content.

On Christmas Eve itself, she'd arranged to finish work at midday. Half her patients had been invited to the party at the manor anyway. During the morning she got a phone call from Mike. 'I have a favour to ask. Could you come over to the manor early this evening? Say about seven? You've done parties there before—I'd like your advice on a couple of things. Come in your party dress in case there isn't time to change. Can you do that for me?'

'Of course,' she said. 'Seven it will be.'

In truth, she was not sure how she felt. A party at the manor but not her party. It seemed really to be the end of an era. She had a bath and dressed slowly in her new gold taffeta gown.

Was this too much? No. She lifted her head proudly. She owed it to the manor itself to pass her much-loved home on graciously.

It was a gorgeous night. The stars shone in a black velvet sky, she could hear the choir practising in the church (she'd been told that they had all been invited up after choir practice), and the air had that sharpness that came with a frost. The snow crunched softly under her feet. She looked down and grinned. Here she was, walking to a party in a gold taffeta gown slit to the thigh—and Wellington boots.

The gates were open. She turned the corner into the drive—and gasped. Tears came to her eyes. At the front of the house on each side of the door a tall Christmas tree stood. Just as they always had at this time of year. And on them were coloured lights—mirrored by the coloured lights in the downstairs windows! Just as they always had been. Even the fairy on top of each tree—this was a re-creation of her childhood!

She felt like a child again, moving up the drive in a dream to stand and gaze up at the trees. It was like a miracle.

Mike must have been looking out for her. He

appeared in the doorway. She had just time to notice that his dinner jacket looked the last word in elegance and that he himself looked more than a little apprehensive. But she had to ask.

'Mike, the Christmas trees, they're wonderful! They're exactly like they used to be. How did you manage it?'

'You're sure you don't mind?'

'Of course I don't mind! How could I mind?'

'You lent Bethany the photograph albums, remember? And I asked Dad what the trees used to look like. And I copied them. Come inside, you must be cold.' He took her arm to draw her into the hall, then angled her towards the cloakroom to one side of the door. 'Can I take your coat? And your...' He looked down, past the seductive slit in the skirt to her Wellingtons.

'Don't you dare laugh. Stand right there without a word while I put my party shoes on.'

'I wouldn't dream of it.' But there was a suspicious wobble in his voice.

'Fibber.' Grace leant on him to change first one foot and then the other. 'There,' she said. 'You can look now.'

The admiration in his eyes was all she'd hoped for. 'May I say you look wonderful?'

'You may.'

'And may I welcome you properly?'

She felt suddenly breathless. 'Properly?'

'Like this.' He took her by the shoulders, his hands warm over the diamanté spaghetti straps, and kissed her. He might have intended to stop before it became a proper, full-on kiss, but the moment their lips met it was heaven.

'You… You said you wanted my advice,' she said faintly.

'Did I?' He seemed as shaken as she was. 'Oh, yes.' He took a deep breath and rotated her gently. 'How does this look to you?'

Grace stood transfixed at the sight of the hall. The old electric fire was long gone, of course, but in its place was a roaring wood fire. To the side of the fireplace was a Christmas tree—with all the big decorations that hadn't fitted on her tree at the cottage! In the centre of the room were two great tables arranged in a T just as they had once been for parties. And around the room were pieces of her own furniture, last seen stored at the Holroyds' farm.

She looked at Mike in bewilderment, feeling tears fill her eyes. 'I don't… How have you…?'

'You told me how lovely it would be to see the hall all grand and festive again. So this is my attempt at showing you. I borrowed your furniture from the farm. I hope you don't mind.'

'Mike, I don't mind! This is so wonderful. I can remember it being just like this and… Thank you, Mike.' Her turn this time to kiss him. But not for long. She wanted to look around, drink it in with her eyes. She only had one tiny, sad thought. This was wonderful—but it wasn't hers any more.

Mike looked a bit more relieved, but there was something else he was nervous about. What else had he done? She was almost afraid to ask.

'You said you used to play party games,' he said. 'I want to try one with you now, a guessing game.' He walked to the big fireplace, its mantelshelf now covered with cards. Above was the mirror that had always been there. Mike really had studied those photos well. But above the mirror was something new—a rolled-up screen, perhaps eight feet long. Mike pulled at a cord, the screen unrolled.

It had a border of Christmas scenes—pictures

of holly, mistletoe, church bells, candles. In the middle there was a message—*Merry Christmas. Welcome home, Grace.*

'Guess what this means?' he said.

She shook her head. 'It's lovely, Mike. But this isn't my home any more. It's yours.'

'It could be your home. If you wanted it.'

'But you're going to live here. You and Bethany.'

He felt in his pocket. 'I said I hadn't wrapped your Christmas present. I lied. The manor is half your present—and this is the other half. If you don't like it we can change it for something else, but I did take a long time picking it.'

Her gave her a small parcel, wrapped in Christmas paper, with a card attached. The card read: *For Grace, with all my love. Mike.*

Grace's heart was beating much too fast. '"With all my love"?'

He put his hand to her face. 'I had to write it before I could say it. It's taken me a while, but I'm there now. With all my love, Grace.'

She tore away the paper with shaking hands, opened the little leather box inside. There was a heart-shaped ruby surrounded by tiny diamonds. She stared at it, speechless, entranced. Then she took it out of the box, held it up so the jewels sparkled and flashed.

He took the ring from her, folded her hand in his. Dimly, dazedly, Grace was aware of Bethany and James at the top of the staircase.

'I love you, Grace. Will you marry me? Marry me and make the manor your home again?'

'I love you too, Mike. Of course I'll marry you.'

She held out her hand, he slid the ring on her finger. The kiss this time was all she had ever wanted, all she had ever hoped for. And was cut short by a delighted little girl in her first long party frock, pelting down the stairs towards them.

'Congratulations, son,' said James, beaming all over his face. 'Grace, I couldn't be more pleased. This is more than a Christmas party now, it's an engagement party! I'll go and break out the champagne!'

Mike nudged them all towards the old kitchen passageway. 'Look up,' he said softly.

Grace smiled. He'd fixed a sprig of mistletoe in the archway. 'Just in case,' he said, and kissed her again.

EPILOGUE

A NEW season. It was the first day of spring, and as beautiful in its way as the winter had been. There was blossom in the fields, the trees were showing new green leaves.

Gardeners had been working hard at Rivercut Manor. By summer the rose garden, herb garden and the shrubbery should be as wonderful as they had been in the manor's heyday.

But they hadn't started to re-lay the new lawn. The old lawn had been left for now—it was just the right size for the marquee that had been erected on it.

This was a village wedding. It seemed as if most of the village were guests, and they all agreed how stunningly beautiful the bride looked in her simple cream silk dress with a full train. Her bouquet was a pretty posy of white and yellow roses. Mike looked handsome in his dark grey morning suit, while Bethany and Chloe made enchanting bridesmaids in long dresses of yellow tulle with circlets of flowers on their heads. The matron of honour was, of course, Natalie, in an amber gown, while James wore his old regimental uniform.

After the service in St Lawrence's, the reception was held in the gardens of Rivercut Manor, the home of the newly married couple. And after a delicious meal, everyone danced long into the night.

'Do you think anyone noticed?' Grace whispered in a rare moment they had alone.

Mike slid his hands over his wife's slender waist. 'There's no sign of Bethany's new brother or sister yet.' Grace's hand moved to cover his, brushing over his third finger where her narrow ring to him nestled snugly alongside Sarah's, both of them making a whole band, and he kissed her tenderly and deeply. 'But do you know how happy it makes me to know he—or she—is there?'

She smiled radiantly up at him. 'As happy as me.'

MEDICAL™

Large Print

Titles for the next six months…

July

POSH DOC, SOCIETY WEDDING	Joanna Neil
THE DOCTOR'S REBEL KNIGHT	Melanie Milburne
A MOTHER FOR THE ITALIAN'S TWINS	Margaret McDonagh
THEIR BABY SURPRISE	Jennifer Taylor
NEW BOSS, NEW-YEAR BRIDE	Lucy Clark
GREEK DOCTOR CLAIMS HIS BRIDE	Margaret Barker

August

EMERGENCY: PARENTS NEEDED	Jessica Matthews
A BABY TO CARE FOR	Lucy Clark
PLAYBOY SURGEON, TOP-NOTCH DAD	Janice Lynn
ONE SUMMER IN SANTA FE	Molly Evans
ONE TINY MIRACLE…	Carol Marinelli
MIDWIFE IN A MILLION	Fiona McArthur

September

THE DOCTOR'S LOST-AND-FOUND BRIDE	Kate Hardy
MIRACLE: MARRIAGE REUNITED	Anne Fraser
A MOTHER FOR MATILDA	Amy Andrews
THE BOSS AND NURSE ALBRIGHT	Lynne Marshall
NEW SURGEON AT ASHVALE A&E	Joanna Neil
DESERT KING, DOCTOR DADDY	Meredith Webber

MEDICAL™

Large Print

October

THE NURSE'S BROODING BOSS	Laura Iding
EMERGENCY DOCTOR AND CINDERELLA	Melanie Milburne
CITY SURGEON, SMALL TOWN MIRACLE	Marion Lennox
BACHELOR DAD, GIRL NEXT DOOR	Sharon Archer
A BABY FOR THE FLYING DOCTOR	Lucy Clark
NURSE, NANNY…BRIDE!	Alison Roberts

November

THE SURGEON'S MIRACLE	Caroline Anderson
DR DI ANGELO'S BABY BOMBSHELL	Janice Lynn
NEWBORN NEEDS A DAD	Dianne Drake
HIS MOTHERLESS LITTLE TWINS	Dianne Drake
WEDDING BELLS FOR THE VILLAGE NURSE	Abigail Gordon
HER LONG-LOST HUSBAND	Josie Metcalfe

December

THE MIDWIFE AND THE MILLIONAIRE	Fiona McArthur
FROM SINGLE MUM TO LADY	Judy Campbell
KNIGHT ON THE CHILDREN'S WARD	Carol Marinelli
CHILDREN'S DOCTOR, SHY NURSE	Molly Evans
HAWAIIAN SUNSET, DREAM PROPOSAL	Joanna Neil
RESCUED: MOTHER AND BABY	Anne Fraser

MILLS & BOON®

X